YUU
MIYAZAKI
ILLUSTRATION BY
okiura
THE ASTERISK WAR
09.
WHISPERS OF A
LONG FAREWELL

"A FORMIDABLE ATTACK BY CONTESTANT BLANCHARD! BUT CONTESTANT ENFIELD HAS DODGED IT BY A FRACTION OF AN INCH!"

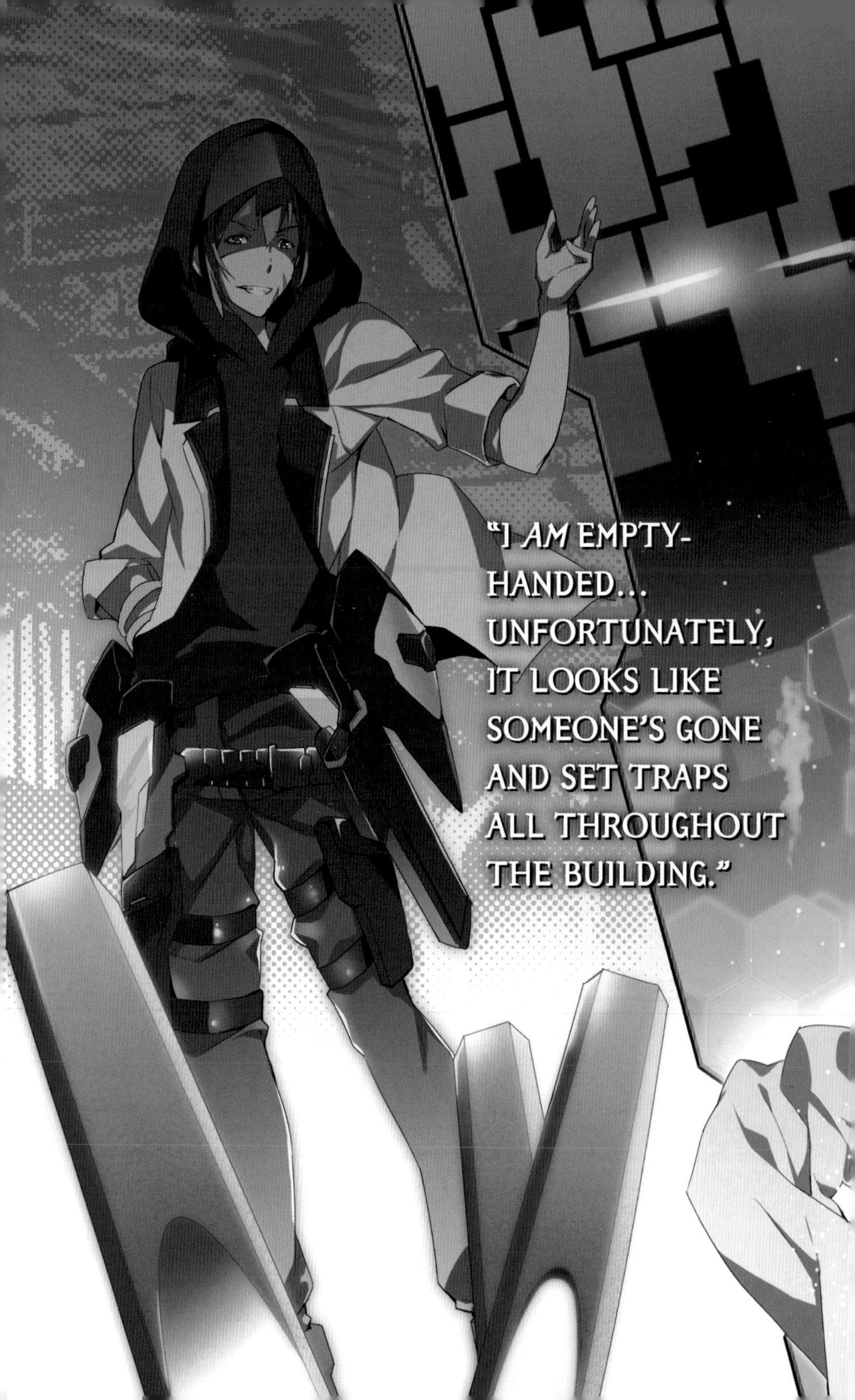
"I *AM* EMPTY-HANDED... UNFORTUNATELY, IT LOOKS LIKE SOMEONE'S GONE AND SET TRAPS ALL THROUGHOUT THE BUILDING."

"...WHAT WAS THAT YOU SAID ABOUT DOING THIS EMPTY-HANDED, EISHIROU?"

"CLAUDIA!"

THE ASTERISK WAR

09. WHISPERS OF A LONG FAREWELL

YUU MIYAZAKI

ILLUSTRATION: OKIURA

NEW YORK

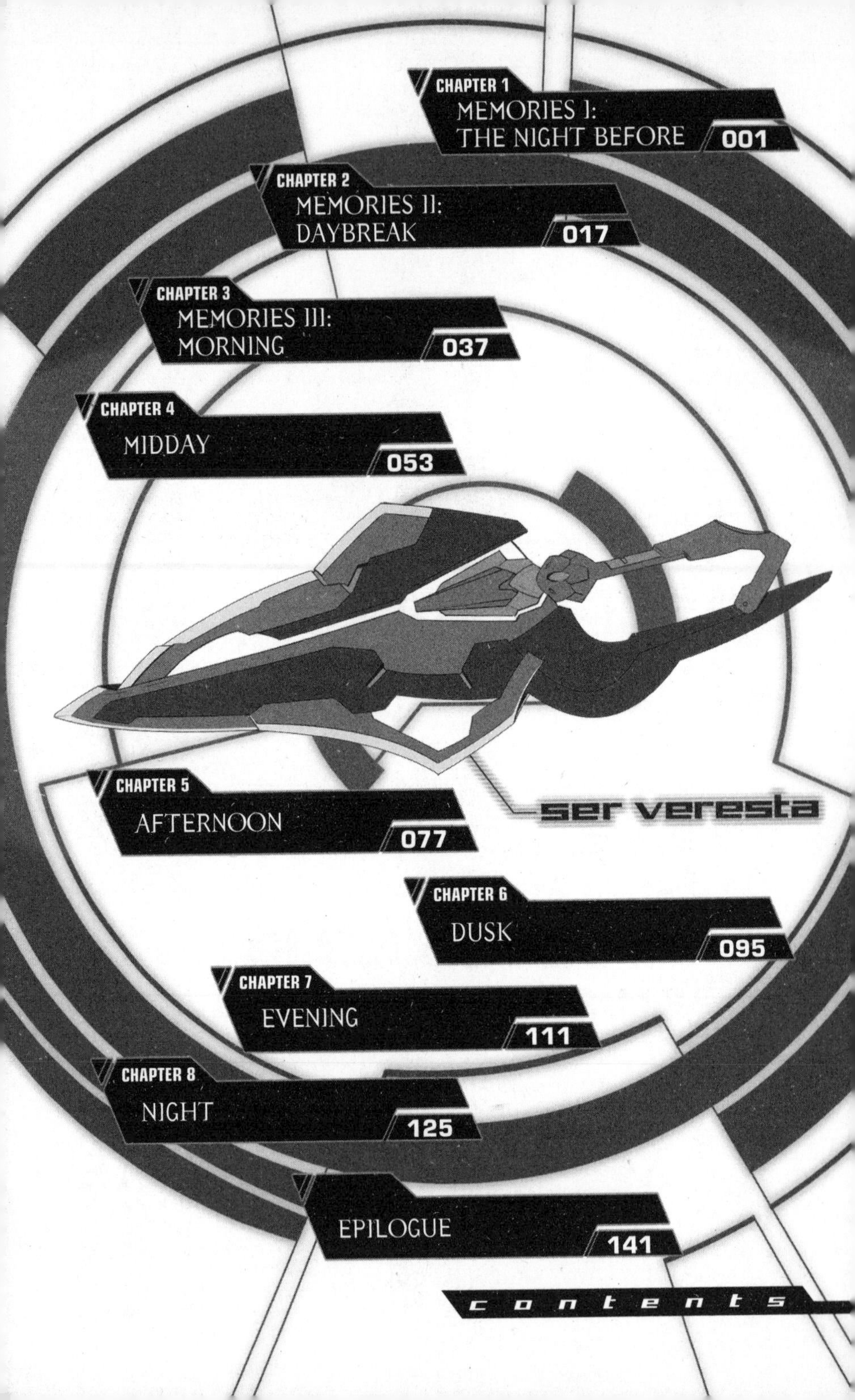

contents

SEIDOUKAN ACADEMY

AYATO AMAGIRI

The protagonist of this work. Wielder of the Ser Veresta. Alias Murakumo.

ALIAS: Gathering Clouds, Murakumo
ORGA LUX: Ser Veresta

JULIS-ALEXIA VON RIESSFELD

Princess of Lieseltania. Ayato's partner for the Phoenix.

ALIAS: the Witch of the Resplendent Flames, Glühen Rose
LUX: Aspera Spina

CLAUDIA ENFIELD

Student council president at Seidoukan Academy. Leader of Team Enfield.

ALIAS: the Commander of a Thousand Visions, Parca Morta
ORGA LUX: Pan-Dora

SAYA SASAMIYA

Ayato's childhood friend. An expert in weaponry and machines.

ALIAS: none yet given
LUX: type 38 Lux grenade launcher Helnekraum, type 34 wave cannon Ark Van Ders Improved Model, and others

KIRIN TOUDOU

Disciple of the Toudou School of swordsmanship with natural talent. Saya's partner for the Phoenix.

ALIAS: the Keen-Edged Tempest, Shippuu Jinrai
LUX: none (wields the katana Senbakiri)

EISHIROU YABUKI

Ayato's roommate. Member of the newspaper club.

LESTER MACPHAIL

Number nine at Seidoukan Academy. Brusque and straightforward but has a deep sense of duty.

RANDY HOOKE

Lester's partner for the Phoenix.

KYOUKO YATSUZAKI

Ayato and company's homeroom teacher.

PREVIOUSLY IN *THE ASTERISK WAR*...

At long last, the Gryps is underway. Thanks to their special training with their homeroom teacher, Kyouko, Team Enfield has proceeded steadily through the tournament. Though Saya and Miluše, the leader of Queenvale's Team Rusalka, briefly went missing after a chance encounter, the two teams squared off in the quarterfinals, and Ayato and company managed to pull through. Meanwhile, Saya, having realized the importance of conveying her true feelings, has resolved to confess everything to Ayato...

characters

THE ASTERISK WAR, Vol. 9
YUU MIYAZAKI

Translation by Haydn Trowell
Cover art by okiura

Yen On
1290 Avenue of the Americas
New York, NY 10104

Visit us at yenpress.com
facebook.com/yenpress
twitter.com/yenpress
yenpress.tumblr.com
instagram.com/yenpress

First Yen On Edition: March 2019

Yen On is an imprint of Yen Press, LLC.
The Yen On name and logo are trademarks of Yen Press, LLC.

The publisher is not responsible for websites (or their content) that are not owned by the publisher.

Library of Congress Cataloging-in-Publication Data
Names: Miyazaki, Yuu, author. | Tanaka, Melissa, translator. |
Trowell, Haydn, translator.
Title: The asterisk war / Yuu Miyazaki ; translation by Melissa Tanaka.
Other titles: Gakusen toshi asterisk. English
Description: First Yen On edition. | New York, NY : Yen On, 2016– |
v. 6–8 translation by Haydn Trowell | Audience: Ages 13 & up.
Identifiers: LCCN 2016023755 | ISBN 9780316315272 (v. 1 : paperback) |
ISBN 9780316398589 (v. 2 : paperback) | ISBN 9780316398602 (v. 3 : paperback) |
ISBN 9780316398626 (v. 4 : paperback) | ISBN 9780316398657 (v. 5 : paperback) |
ISBN 9780316398671 (v. 6 : paperback) | ISBN 9780316398695 (v. 7 : paperback) |
ISBN 9780316398718 (v. 8 : paperback) | ISBN 9781975302801 (v. 9 : paperback)
Subjects: CYAC: Science fiction. | BISAC: FICTION / Science Fiction / Adventure.
Classification: LCC PZ7.1.M635 As 2016 | DDC [Fic]—dc23
LC record available at https://lccn.loc.gov/2016023755

ISBNs: 978-1-9753-0280-1 (paperback)
978-1-9753-0428-7 (ebook)

1 3 5 7 9 10 8 6 4 2

LSC-C

Printed in the United States of America

CHAPTER 1
MEMORIES I: THE NIGHT BEFORE

As a child, Claudia had always assumed she would walk the same path through life as her parents.

She was a prodigy by every definition of the word, gifted with exceptional intelligence and physical ability. She was particularly astute when it came to carefully reading the people around her, easily intuiting what they desired and despised. Moreover, she was endowed with such a fine control over words and mannerisms as to be able to create within others any impression of herself that she so desired.

Indeed, she ought to have been sufficiently qualified for such a future out of both raw ability and breeding. (Her family status was particularly important in the European integrated enterprise foundations.) It shouldn't have been at all surprising to see her rise to the upper echelons of the IEF realm to sit among the handful of people who held in their hands the power to change the world.

That was, if she hadn't been born a Genestella.

One day, things would change. The number of Genestella—or rather, the percentage of Genestella within the general population—was increasing, albeit slowly. In a few decades perhaps, or at the very most a few centuries, a time would come when the world's Genestella would shake off the shackles of being a feared minority.

But that time had yet to come.

In today's world, Genestella were regarded as little more than freaks of nature. No matter how talented they were, no matter their achievements, there was no place for them in the upper reaches of the system.

Claudia's parents, Isabella and Nicholas, had, of course, understood that immediately, and so had Claudia by the time she was ten. And yet, upon that realization, she hadn't succumbed to discouragement or despair.

She had no particularly strong desires, nor was she chasing any particular goals.

She existed in a place far removed from such things as wants or passion.

That was the kind of person Claudia Enfield was.

"Hiiyah!"

A razor-sharp sword swept before her.

Her opponent's gleaming golden locks danced through the air as she lunged forward, mimicking the way her own golden mane appeared before her eyes as she leaped out of the way.

"A formidable attack by contestant Blanchard! But contestant Enfield has dodged it by a fraction of an inch! Such a fierce contest for the final match of this Rondo Versailles!"

There were many fighting tournaments that ranked below the Festa, but the Rondo, held in several western European countries, was among the most famous. Entry was restricted to those under thirteen years of age, and there were far stricter safety requirements than the Festa. All contestants were obliged to wear padded armor, only specially designated weapons were permitted—each of them Luxes with their power output set to their minimum level—and there was a complete prohibition on the use of special abilities. In short, it was the closest thing to a Festa intended for children. That was also why a point system had been introduced—one gained points for landing a strike on an opponent's armor, with the winner being the contestant who scored the most.

There could be remarkable differences in the rate of physical growth among Genestella—particularly with regard to physique, muscular development, and the amount of one's prana. While the situation tended to even out by the time children reached puberty, before that, the differences in prana levels were particularly evident, which meant that a person's ability to adequately defend themselves could be limited. As such, safety measures were a necessity for such tournaments.

That caution wasn't, however, due to concern for the children's own well-being. Rather, the intention was to avoid damaging the goods up for appraisal.

Most tournaments that ranked below the Festa didn't have much commercial value. Rather, they functioned more as opportunities to show off new talent to the various schools in Asterisk.

...You need to be at a high level to be shipped off to those exhibition shows that pass themselves off as schools, Claudia reflected as she dodged her opponent, who continued to flow toward her gracefully, as if in the middle of a dance.

That opponent—Laetitia Blanchard—had, like her, made it all the way to the final at the age of nine.

"Grrr, why won't you stay still?!" Laetitia raged, thrusting her blade upward.

Claudia, though, parried the blow with her own short-sword-type Lux, before letting out a kindly laugh. "You're improving, Laetitia."

"Rargh! Why are you always so calm?! Take this!"

Her sword carved through the air at an unexpected angle, coming straight for Claudia's chest. The two had crossed swords countless times before, but this was the first time Claudia had seen Laetitia use such a move.

Laetitia curled her lips in faint smile, as if assured of victory.

However—

"What?!"

Claudia swung her body with all her strength, letting the attack rush right past her, before she used her own sword to lash out in a quick flurry at the armor protecting Laetitia's legs, arms, and chest.

Almost immediately, the sound announcing the end of the match echoed across the stage.

Claudia, flashing her stunned opponent a gentle smile, deactivated her Lux. "Sorry. That last move was a close one."

"Argh…!" Laetitia bit her lip, her face turning red in indignation. "Y-you just got lucky! Don't let it get to your head!"

"Luck? I see… You're probably right. Including the practice matches, that's seven in my favor now. You must be having an unlucky run, Laetitia."

"Rrgh… Th-that's…"

"But victory always requires some degree of luck, so might I suggest factoring that into your strategy next time?"

Laetitia, angry and at a complete loss for words, looked upset enough to break down in tears.

Claudia, however, still smiling, held out her hand. "…That said, luck may be in your favor next time, too. If that happens, please don't be too hard on me."

"—!"

Laetitia turned around for a moment to wipe her eyes, before spinning back toward Claudia to take her hand. "Th-that's right! It's unladylike not to praise one's opponent… Congratulations, Claudia. But next time, I'm definitely, *definitely* going to win!" she declared, her grin a little forced.

Her smile was unable to completely conceal her feelings, but it wasn't clear whether that was from the inability to tolerate the humiliation of defeat or her jealousy and envy toward the victor. It was clear, however, that her praise was honest.

Claudia had to admit that she liked that side of Laetitia.

The two girls shook hands to the cheers of the crowd. Even if the Rondo didn't have much commercial value, it was, in its own way, afforded a great deal of attention. So many spectators had come to watch, in fact, that there hadn't even been enough seats for everyone.

"This year, we've seen the same two contestants fight off in the final as we did last time! And like last year, the winner is once again contestant Enfield!"

Claudia broke into an amused smile at the commentator's voice. "And besides, you weren't able to use your abilities, so I don't really think of myself as having beaten you," she whispered to Laetitia afterward.

Laetitia was a Strega, capable of creating and controlling brilliant wings of light. She was still honing it into specialized offensive and defensive forms, but there was no mistaking that even in its current stage, it was an incredibly powerful ability. The fact that using such abilities during the Rondo was prohibited meant Laetitia had fought with something of a handicap.

"I-I'm not so shameful as to blame my loss on the rules!" she stammered.

Laetitia herself was no doubt aware that it wasn't entirely luck that had decided the outcome; but her pride, it seemed, wouldn't let her admit that out loud.

"Besides, one of these days, I'll face you in a more suitable place, and then I shall defeat you!" she continued.

"Are you thinking of Asterisk, then?"

"Well, I mean, you'll be there, too," Laetitia replied, as if it were a predetermined fact.

"Yes, that's right... I suppose."

Claudia herself wasn't entirely clear where she saw herself in the future.

There was no doubt that the majority of people who participated in the Rondo hoped to one day enter Asterisk. For better or for worse, the Academic City in the Far East was the only place in the world where being a Genestella had any real meaning.

That said, it wasn't as if Claudia herself was particularly fixated on it. Whether it was entering the Rondo or polishing her skills, she had merely found herself caught up in the flow of events. She felt no more and no less about it than that.

Looking at her own talents objectively, there was no mistaking that she would be able to distinguish herself at Asterisk. At the same time, however, she also knew there were countless people hidden throughout the world with greater talent than she had.

Moreover, crossing that wall wouldn't be an easy task, no matter one's determination and training.

If she did have the motivation to climb, there might have been some meaning to her going there. Unfortunately, however, she wasn't so foolish as to think she could challenge the way the world was put together.

"By the way, Laetitia... I've been wondering for a while now, but what is it you're doing with your manner of speech?" Claudia asked, changing the topic.

"Huh? U-uh, that's..." The other girl looked away, blushing.

Laetitia usually had a slightly informal, childlike way of speaking. Now, however, her tone was unusually polite, almost overdone.

"Y-yes, well... The other day, I met a certain brother and sister... They were so wise and noble, I thought—well, I thought that they were so wonderful—and that I'd like to be like them, too, if I could, and get closer to them...," Laetitia explained, fidgeting nervously.

She must have been inspired to change her own character, Claudia thought. Given her somewhat naive way of thinking, that wasn't particularly unusual, and yet—

"Do you perhaps mean the Fairclough siblings?"

"O-oh!" Laetitia said, her eyes lighting up. "Do you, ah, know them, perhaps?"

"Not at all. I've never met them. I have heard rumors, though."

While they might not have appeared in public events such as the Rondo, it was a well-known fact that there were two siblings, brother and sister, from the famous Fairclough family, both of whom excelled in swordsmanship. Moreover, in spite of their lack of public appearances, there was enough consistency to the rumors about their skills that they did seem to be the real deal.

"Ah, so that last technique of yours... Did you learn it from them?"

"W-well, you could...say that...," Laetitia replied, scratching at her cheek, her expression somewhere between bashfulness and pride. "A-anyway, they said they'll be going to Asterisk, too, to Gallardworth, like me."

Both the Fairclough family and the Blanchard family belonged to the same faction within Elliott-Pound, the integrated enterprise foundation that operated Saint Gallardworth Academy.

"You'll be going to Seidoukan, right? I'll look forward to seeing you in Asterisk," Laetitia said with a defiant grin, very much like the matter had already been determined.

"Hmm… One would think so, wouldn't they?" Claudia's answer, however, was accompanied by her usual vague smile.

Things might end up happening that way, or they might not.

For her, it made little difference.

*

"If I can, I want to be by your side forever," Saya said shyly in the light of the setting sun.

Ayato, standing across from her, merely stared at her in mute astonishment.

"It's okay. You can give me your answer later… I just wanted to tell you," she added, before quickly turning around and rushing back in the direction of the girls' dormitory.

She quickened her pace, until finally she reached an area out of Ayato's line of sight. There, she stepped off the path and hid in the shadow of a tree.

Leaning against the trunk, she put her hands together and raised them to her chest with a sigh.

Her face, with cheeks flushed and eyes shut tight, was truly innocent.

It looked like her decision to come out with that confession had been quite the momentous occasion for her.

"Well now, Sasamiya's more maidenly than she lets on," Eishirou murmured to himself, high in the branches of the trees above her.

Of course, he had been too far away to clearly hear what they had said. Strictly speaking, he had read their lips.

"But this is getting pretty interesting, huh? I mean, just look at that stupid gaping look he's making." He glanced back toward Ayato, who, it seemed, was so astounded that he still hadn't moved from where he was standing.

Eishirou was hiding in a corner of one of the groves of trees that provided some greenery to Seidoukan's wide grounds. Autumn might have arrived, but the leaves that hid him hadn't yet changed color and were still a verdant green.

"Hmm... But not asking him for his response—that won't do. What on earth was she thinking?" he muttered to himself.

Neither Saya nor Ayato were used to dealing with matters of the heart. From Eishirou's perspective, there was nothing more irritating than having to watch them fumble their way through their feelings blindly.

There was no mistaking, however, that this would certainly throw a wrench into the plans for Ayato's relationships with the other girls.

"Well, I guess I'm gonna have to report it to the prez. Maybe I'll finally be able to see her make a cute little surprised face?" he continued, before shaking his head doubtfully.

He couldn't even imagine what a surprised Claudia might look like.

"Maybe I'll give it to the newspaper club instead? But then, the club prez doesn't really like this sort of thing anyway. And I'm not gonna be able to see her too easily right now, either." With that, he took his mobile from his pocket, about to call Claudia, when—

"Good grief, so you're using your techniques for voyeurism, are you?" a low, hoarse voice said from behind him. "I thought you'd grown up a little, but it looks like you haven't changed at all, *Eishirou*."

"!" Eishirou jumped up, spinning around and reflexively pulling out a dagger-type Lux—but he was already surrounded by several figures, all seeming to seep out from the shadows around him. With the exception of their eyes, they were masked and clothed entirely in black, their identities hidden so thoroughly that it was impossible to so much as tell their ages or genders.

Eishirou, however, knew precisely who they were—especially the man with the hoarse voice.

"...Well, if it isn't my dear father. I didn't think you'd be here... You look well," he returned with an ironic smile, trying to ignore the sweat that had begun to run down his forehead.

His father—Bujinsai Yabuki—was dressed the same as the others, the only exception being that his face was uncovered. He was a middle-aged man of medium build, his face so wrinkled that the creases seemed to have been carved into his flesh, his hair combed down flat and smooth, his eyebrows pure white.

"Don't say what you don't mean," the older man said with an affected sigh as he sat cross-legged on the branch behind him. "Don't think I haven't heard that you're still tottering about without a care in the world. It's disgraceful."

"Oh? I don't know what you're talking about," Eishirou answered glibly, preparing his Lux as he carefully scanned his surroundings.

"Did you think you could take us all for fools? Despite joining Shadowstar, you're still taking your own jobs and associating with outsiders."

"No, no, not at all—that's not a fair accusation. I mean, I might have made a few acquaintances here and there, but that's simply for work. Just building up a bit of influence, wouldn't you say?"

"So the little babe is going to talk to me about work, is he? How pathetic. Do you even realize that it's precisely because we never serve two masters that we've been able to survive this long?"

...I wonder whether you realize that's why I left the village, Eishirou retorted mentally, his chin resting on his hand as he flashed Bujinsai a fawning smirk.

Eishirou's clan, the Yabuki, was, in short, a secretive paramilitary organization that specialized in ninjutsu, the ancient Japanese art of stealth, camouflage, and sabotage. Additionally, they belonged to and preserved a bloodline that, under the influence of a sacred piece of urm-manadite that had come to earth long before the Invertia, had long since diverged from the surrounding population. Only two such groups remained in Japan—the Yabuki and the Umenokouji.

"Now, now, you didn't come all this way just to lecture me, did you? No, you must be here on some kind of job, right?" Eishirou asked, furtively retreating as he took in his surroundings.

The five figures closest to him were probably the Kinoe, the most elite members of the clan. On top of that, he could sense close to another ten individuals lurking somewhere nearby.

"That's what I'm on my way to find out."

Jobs were always issued to the head of the clan in person—that was how it had always been.

"So I'm guessing they specifically asked you to bring such a large party?"

"You could say that."

Today, the clan accepted jobs only from the IEF Galaxy—or more specifically, from its highest executives—who referred to them by the inane name of "the Anglicism the Night Emits." In a certain way, they were to Galaxy what Shadowstar was to Seidoukan. Shadowstar, however, was permitted to act only within Asterisk, and it recruited from the general student body, while the Yabuki were entrusted with carrying out Galaxy's secret maneuverings irrespective of where that might take them. In a way, Shadowstar's activities could be said to comprise a subset of the Yabuki's, although in Shadowstar's favor, there were also naturally things that only students could access.

Of course, the foundation wasn't solely reliant on the Yabuki. It also had its own paramilitary brigades and special forces that functioned under its direct control—in addition to its own intelligence services, which worked tirelessly to gain an edge over the other foundations' similar branches in endless, secretive feuding.

There was no mistaking, however, that the highest executives—essentially Galaxy itself—viewed the Yabuki with particular esteem.

"Once we accept a job, we carry it out all the way to the end, without letting any personal feelings get in the way. Which is why, before we begin, I want to ask you how you fit into it all."

"..."

That was enough for Eishirou to ascertain just what kind of job his father was about to be entrusted with. "I see, I see. So Galaxy's finally decided to take care of the prez, huh?"

"We haven't received it yet," Bujinsai answered.

He was no doubt merely feigning ignorance—there was no way he would mobilize the clan like this if he didn't already know what it would entail.

"But it does seem like that's the case," he added, a cold light flashing in his eyes, a dangerous glimmer bordering on bloodlust.

Sensing the sudden chill, so strong and arising so quickly that it was like a blade of ice piercing his heart, Eishirou instinctively leaped away from Bujinsai in order to break through the encircling Kinoe.

"Ugh!"

And yet, as if having anticipated his movements, the Kinoe immediately reached out to him, trying to pen him in.

Eishirou managed to break out of the trap by striking the leg of one of the five Kinoe, sending them crashing, then jumped over another figure and twisted its neck. Leaping away once more, he drove a powerful kick into the back of the neck of another figure, which had been coming toward him from the side.

The remaining Kinoe, however, paid no heed to their fallen comrades. He was getting ready to lash out at another of them with his dagger when a heavy weight slammed into him from the side, pressing him against the trunk of the tree.

"Oh? So you can take down three Kinoe all by yourself now? You've been working on your skills, I take it?" Bujinsai noted, impressed, as he stroked his chin.

With that, the three Kinoe whom Eishirou had taken down jumped back to their feet as if nothing had happened, positioning themselves beside him in silence.

They didn't look to have suffered any damage; in fact, his attacks didn't seem to have done anything at all. Eishirou knew firsthand just how skilled the Kinoe were, and so while it might take them some time, considering that there were five of them, there was no question that they would be able to subdue him if they so desired.

But that wasn't the Yabuki's way of doing things. No matter the situation, their highest priority was to reach the target as promptly and as surely as possible.

Just thinking about it all reminded him how much he hated them.

"Listen up, boy! I know how fond you are of that girl, Seidoukan's student council president. But you had better not do anything stupid. That's my warning to you as your father."

"...Well, thanks." Eishirou, still being held down with a force strong enough that it risked breaking his arm, could move only his face to glare back at Bujinsai, towering above him.

Casting his gaze as best he could at his surroundings, he could make out several spell charms marked with complex symbols placed here and there to ward off intruders.

How diligent of them... I guess I can't count on them to let down their guard...

Eishirou, giving up, relaxed his body. Nothing would be gained from trying to resist them now.

"We might have our disagreements, but I do have a certain level of respect for you and your talents. It would be a shame to lose them over something like this. Do you understand what I'm saying?"

"In a way."

Bujinsai could say what he wanted, but Eishirou knew well enough that if he was to get in the way of their mission, his father wouldn't hesitate to break his neck.

"And so?"

"Haah..." As he watched that cold glimmer return to Bujinsai's eyes, Eishirou let out a resigned sigh. "I *certainly* am fond of the prez. But I'm attached to my own life span a little more."

"That's a good attitude to have."

And with that, the force with which he had been held back suddenly abated.

Eishirou rose to his feet, brushing his hand against his clothes as if sweeping away dust.

Bujinsai and the Kinoe had completely vanished.

The evening sun had almost completely fallen beneath the horizon, a forlorn twilight settling over the trees.

"...*Tch.*" Eishirou clicked his tongue in exasperation and, after a slight hesitation, reached for his mobile.

"I can keep a sense of duty at least, Pops," Eishirou muttered as he entered Claudia's number and set the device to voice only.

*

"...Whew..."

Ayato, wiping at his still wet hair with a bath towel, let out a long sigh as he sat down on his bed.

All he could think about was Saya—and what she had said to him.

He liked her, too, of course, and he knew for a fact that her intentions were honest. However, he had only ever thought of her as an extended family member, never anything more.

"...Or maybe that's just what I wanted to think," he murmured to the empty room as he fell backward onto the bed.

Eishirou hadn't come back yet—although there was nothing unusual about that, considering that there were no classes during the Festa—giving him the perfect opportunity to try to put his thoughts in order.

Having been reunited with her in Asterisk after all those years, it was almost as if she hadn't changed at all since their childhood, when they had spent almost every passing day by each other's side.

That had made him incredibly happy.

But if she had asked him to give her an answer on the spot, he would have found himself hard-pressed to know what to say.

Right now, he had a wish that he wanted to see fulfilled: to be able to wake his sister, Haruka, from her unending sleep.

Most of his thoughts were occupied by his drive to fulfill that wish, but given the seriousness of Saya's feelings, she deserved no less than his full attention.

Saya no doubt knew that as well, which must have been why she had said that he didn't have to give her his answer immediately.

"Well, I guess I'll have to take her up on that offer..."

Once he had put everything in order, he would be able to face her properly and give her his full attention.

And in order to be able to do that, he would have to focus first on winning the next match.

"...Right!" He slapped his hands against his cheeks to fire himself up, when his mobile, which he had flung beside him on his bed, began to ring. "Huh? Again?"

It was already past midnight.

He opened an air-window, and Claudia's face appeared before him.

"Good evening, Ayato. I'm terribly sorry to call you this late, but do you have a moment?"

"Ah, I don't mind... But is it urgent?"

They were due to have a strategy meeting with the other members of Team Enfield in the morning, so if it wasn't pressing, they would be able to discuss it then.

"Yes, I'm afraid so." Claudia's expression, devoid of her usual smile, was unusually serious.

"...Okay. What is it?"

"Yes, well, you see— Is it true that Ms. Sasamiya confessed to you?"

"Wh-wha—?!" Ayato found himself blurting. "H-hold on a minute! How you do know that?"

"I am *the student council president."*

"What does that have to do with anything?!"

She might have been well-informed, but this was something else entirely.

"Putting that aside, I'm also deeply concerned about what kind of response you might have given her."

"...I don't have any obligation to tell you that."

It was, after all, a private matter.

"Yes, you're quite right. However...we're still in the middle of the Gryps, are we not? If anything was to happen that might interfere with our teamwork, that would be a cause for serious alarm to us all."

It was certainly difficult to argue with that.

"As the team's representative, I have to ask."

"...That's just an excuse," he replied sullenly, glaring at her. If she already knew that much, however, there was no use remaining silent.

"I haven't given her one yet. She said I can give her my answer later, so I was planning to do it after everything's over and done with."

"Is that so...?" Claudia fell silent, nodding calmly. "*...Ms. Sasamiya really is quite impressive,*" she murmured, as if talking to herself.

"Claudia...?" Ayato asked, sensing something out of place in her actions.

He couldn't put it into words, but whatever it was, it had stirred a deep-rooted sense of uneasiness somewhere inside him.

"I understand, Ayato. Thank you for telling me the truth... Well then, see you tomorrow." Before Ayato could respond, she flashed him her usual smile, signaling the end of the conversation.

"Yeah. See you then," Ayato grudgingly replied before the air-window snapped shut, filling the room with silence. "...I guess I'll have to ask her tomorrow."

His vague sense of apprehension was still bothering him, but there was nothing he could do about it right then.

He turned his gaze out through the window, toward the cloud-covered night sky. Though so spectacular just a few hours ago, both the moon and the stars were now completely hidden from view.

"Right, it's supposed to rain tomorrow..."

He pulled the curtain shut in silence, hoping the weather wouldn't turn out too bad.

CHAPTER 2
MEMORIES II: DAYBREAK

"Oh, yes, Claudia. What do you say we go watch the next Lindvolus?" Nicholas asked her suddenly one morning, some time after her victory at the Rondo Versailles. They were having breakfast together, and he was waiting for the servant to finish pouring him a cup of tea.

"The Lindvolus?" Claudia repeated, momentarily setting aside her apple compote to glance at him.

The residence was built in the Gothic Revival style and had been relocated from the town of Tiverton. It was practically overflowing with antique furniture and furnishings, and it was filled with pristine white tablecloths and matching tableware of every possible size and shape, all according to Nicholas's tastes. He no doubt thought that these nostalgic flavors lent him a certain noble character.

"I don't mind... Although, it is rather sudden," Claudia replied.

"I was invited to attend. It's a rare opportunity, so I thought you might both accompany me," Isabella, whose utilitarianism stood in sharp contrast to the indulgences of her husband, said with a calm, gentle smile.

"Well now, that *is* rare."

As far as Claudia could remember, her family had only ever gone on outings together on a handful of occasions.

It was, moreover, rare in itself for her family to all eat breakfast in one another's company. While the situation was different with her father, Claudia could easily count the number of times she shared breakfast with her mother each year.

"I'm going to be rather busy starting next year, and given my position, I won't be free to go where I like. Which means that it will be difficult for me to watch the Festa." Isabella was already close to occupying one of the top executive positions at Galaxy. If she was promoted again, what little time she had left to herself would no doubt all but disappear.

"And it will be good for you to get a taste of Asterisk for yourself, don't you think?" Nicholas added.

"Well, I suppose..."

Her parents, it seemed, were trying to show their hesitant daughter the path through life they wanted her to take. In that case, she couldn't turn them down without a good reason.

"We aren't saying you have to go to Asterisk. Just think of it as taking a look. The choice is, after all, up to you." Her father might have come across as trying to push her toward making a decision, but Claudia understood that he was only trying to look out for her.

Isabella, however, probably hadn't realized that. Normally, for her, a child at the Festa would be nothing more than a nuisance. The fact that she wasn't resisting her husband on the issue suggested that she, too, was indeed sparing some thought to her daughter's future.

In short, her father and mother both loved her, each in their own ways.

And Claudia loved them both, too.

Which was why—

"Thank you very much," she answered with a bright smile.

Though she might have appeared so to others, Claudia wasn't actually a hesitant child—rather, she neither felt strongly nor had any particular attachment to the potential future paths she might travel down.

To its fans, the Lindvolus was known as the Festa of Festas.

There were several reasons for its high esteem, including that it was the very first of the three extant forms of the tournament and that it determined the results for the entire season. But by far the most significant reason was its showcasing individuals, deciding the strongest student of the day through a tournament.

In the past, the title of Prior, awarded to the student who scored the most points in a given season, had been the ultimate glory. However, as each of Asterisk's schools developed more elaborate strategies for the Festa, they began to have students participate only in those tournaments for which they were best suited, and individual students ended up scoring less points in each season overall. On top of that, the contest for the title of Prior had ended up causing considerable strife within the various schools. Ultimately, those factors led to the title itself having been abolished close to twenty years ago. As such, the Lindvolus had come to take its place as the most highly valued of the Festa's activities.

"...I see," Claudia murmured to herself in one of the Sirius Dome's VIP rooms as the contest unfolded before her. "This is what one should expect from the Festa. It's on a completely different level than the lower categories."

The tournament was still in its first round, but each of the contestants who had entered the stage so far had considerable skill. Claudia had, of course, watched videos of past Festas, but there was no comparison to seeing it for herself.

"Well, the most notable players are assigned to matches here at the Sirius Dome, so those at the other venues will probably be somewhat less exciting," Nicholas commented.

"Hmm. That reminds me, there's supposed to be a promising young talent from Seidoukan coming up in the next match," Isabella remarked.

Claudia's parents, sitting on either side of her, looked like they had come to watch the Festa several times before. That said, neither seemed to be particularly interested. As Galaxy executives, their attendance was more a matter of courtesy than anything else.

"A promising talent?" Claudia asked.

"He defeated a Page One in a recent official ranking match, taking their place. And it looks like he got his hands on a particularly powerful Orga Lux recently, too," Nicholas answered, consulting a small air-window.

"What kind of Orga Lux?"

Claudia wasn't completely ignorant when it came to Asterisk. If that student had acquired it just recently, then they had probably put in an application for it after becoming a Page One.

"I think it's called the Pan-Dora or something like that," her father answered, seemingly disinterested. "It seems to have some sort of precognition ability..."

"Oh? That sounds rather extraordinary."

If that was true, someone with that kind of ability would be all but sure to win unless their opponent's skills considerably outpaced their own.

"It sounds like it demands a high cost, however. That would explain why no one's been able to use it properly until now. I wonder how this newcomer will fare?"

"...I expect he'll have a hard time. That professor's creations all have their own little quirks."

"Hmm?" Claudia wondered, looking toward her mother. Isabella's manner of speaking had seemed to contain a hint of prophecy.

At that moment, however, the announcer's voice echoed across the arena, and the contestants began to enter the stage from the gates at either side.

According to the data in the air-window beside her, the one who entered from the west gate was from Queenvale. She seemed to be ranked, but to Claudia, at least, she didn't look like the kind of contestant who could hope to make it very far. The student entering from the east gate, on the other hand, was the promising young talent from Seidoukan—but no sooner had he entered the stage than a disquieting murmur ran through the crowd.

"Ah, just as I thought." Isabella, seemingly disappointed, put a hand against her cheek.

The young man was clearly in a poor state. He proceeded onto the stage with weak, tottering steps, and his face projected in the huge air-windows that ringed the stadium seemed sapped of energy. His eyes were hollow, his cheeks sunken like those of an invalid. It was obvious enough that he was in no condition to put forth a satisfactory effort.

Perhaps spurred on by nothing more than a will to fight, he advanced slowly onto the stage, activating the Orga Lux he held in his hands. The twin blades, decorated with designs that looked unsettlingly like moving eyeballs, began to let out a vaguely ominous aura.

"—?!"

At that moment, a shock ran through Claudia's body, as if she had been struck by a bolt of lightning.

She felt as if the eyes engraved in the hilts of those twin blades had fixed her with a piercing glare. But it wasn't only that. The swords, of course, had no moving parts capable of forming expressions, but she couldn't shake the feeling that they had somehow broken into a wide smirk.

"...!"

Before she knew it, she had jumped to her feet.

"What is it, Claudia?" Nicholas asked with a quizzical look.

Claudia, still reeling from whatever it was that had come upon her, hesitated for a brief moment but soon regained her composure, shaking her head gently. "No, I'm sorry. It's nothing..."

Isabella, however, fixed her with a faint smile, as if seeing right through her. "Maybe you felt something, from the Orga Lux, perhaps?"

"...What do you mean?"

"That kind of thing happens sometimes with Orga Luxes. They choose their users, not the other way around... And apparently, at such times, one can feel as if the Orga Lux is smiling at them."

"..."

Claudia stared back at her mother in silence, before breaking her gaze and heading toward the door.

"H-hey, Claudia...?" came Nicholas's perplexed voice.

"I'm going to get some fresh air," Claudia responded as she stepped out of the VIP room.

She heard later that the young man from Seidoukan suffered an overwhelming defeat.

*

"...I see. Good work." Having listened to their report, Ernest Fairclough thanked the three men standing before him and then let out a deep sigh.

The three men each wore the white gilded robes and geometrical masks of Inquisitors from Sinodomius, Saint Gallardworth Academy's intelligence organization.

Sinodomius was said to be the only intelligence organization associated with Asterisk's six schools that concerned itself purely with collecting information, while refraining from all other kinds of clandestine activity. As student council president, however, Ernest was well aware that that was merely the group's public face. It was precisely through his use of them, and because they were willing to do what had to be done, that he was able to hold sway over all of Gallardworth, the good and the bad.

However, that often wasn't an easy thing to reconcile with the cost demanded by his Orga Lux, the Lei-Glems.

But now, after hearing the Inquisitors' report, he couldn't help worrying about what kind of effect it could have on his blade.

"Good morning," a voice said, followed by three knocks on the door to his office. "I'm coming in, Ernest."

Laetitia Blanchard, the student council vice president, entered the room. Behind her was the other vice president, Kevin Holst; the student council secretary, Percival Gardner; and the student council treasurer, Lionel Karsch.

These five individuals, Ernest included, formed Saint Gallardworth Academy's student council, in addition to the academy's top five Page Ones.

While there were also, of course, support staff that handled much of the necessary administrative work, Gallardworth was essentially governed by these five individuals.

"Come on, Ernest, you could have just left it to us and taken a day off for once. What do you think you're doing, working this early in the morning? You should try looking after yourself—" Laetitia, known for her charitableness and refined character, swallowed her words upon setting eyes on the three robed men, her face twisting in a deep frown. Her hatred for the Inquisitors knew no bounds.

She looked away from the three figures as they filed out of the room, before finally turning to Ernest once they had closed the door behind them. "...Something must have happened for three of them to come here at this time of day. What is it?"

It was no exaggeration to call the hour early. The morning sun had only just begun to peek through the window on the room's east side, accompanied by the chirps of birds announcing the beginning of a new day.

"Let's not worry about that now," Ernest said, dodging the question and turning to the beautiful young woman dressed in a boy's uniform. "More importantly, your report, Percival."

"Understood," she began, before reading out the list of the day's tasks. "On this morning's schedule, the first task is to look over several documents, confirm the next official ranking-match pairings, address the supplementary budget of the Association of Humanities Clubs, evaluate and respond to the requests carried over from yesterday, and..."

"...Looks like today's gonna be another long one. If only I'd been able to get some proper sleep," Kevin said, putting his hands behind his head and letting out an exaggerated yawn while Percival continued with her report.

Kevin was a slim, handsome man, and, unusually for one of Gallardworth's knights, of somewhat frivolous character. Moreover, he was involved in a seemingly endless litany of stories involving romances with women both within and outside of the academy. But historically speaking, at least, that sort of thing went hand in hand with knighthood, so it couldn't exactly be said that he was unworthy of the title.

Moreover, Ernest couldn't deny that there was a part of him that liked Kevin's lighthearted approach to life.

That personality was a stark contrast to that of the large man standing next to him. "...You shameless fool. Can't you hold yourself straight in the mornings at least?" Lionel scoffed, looking down at him sternly.

Lionel, in sharp contrast to Kevin, was serious to a fault, the epitome of the kind of person who forever remained sober and honest. Graced with a gallant fighting style that had earned him the alias of Royal Spear, he paid such meticulous attention to form and strategy, even in every aspect of his own daily life, that he could well be called the cornerstone of the student council.

"What do you expect? I had to go to three separate parties yesterday, so of course, I'm exhausted."

"I don't have the slightest interest in your obscene private life, but it will reflect on all of us if it interferes with your duties."

"As a knight, I have a responsibility to answer when called on by a lady. Aren't you the one who's taking that a little lightly, Leo?"

"Are you trying to talk your way out of things again?"

"Not really. I'm just saying it like it is."

Just as the two men were about to truly start quarreling, the sound of a gunshot suddenly rang out.

"...Did either of you hear a single thing I just said?" Percival had activated her pistol-type Lux, firing it directly into the ceiling. "Next time, I'll be aiming at you," she warned them both coldly.

Kevin and Lionel fell silent, waving their hands in surrender. They knew full well just how serious she was when it came to her reports.

"...Got it, Percy. My—our bad, right, Leo?"

"...Exactly. Sorry about that, Gardner."

"Then I shall continue," Percival replied, returning to her list of tasks as if nothing had happened. Her Lux, however, remained activated and ready for use.

Laetitia, on the other hand, glanced up at the fresh hole in the ceiling tiredly. "...Why on earth does she have to be so quick to pull the trigger...?" she murmured under her breath.

"Ha-ha... Well, that's just how she is," Ernest replied with a quiet laugh.

And it was no doubt precisely because that was how she was that the Holy Grail had chosen her as its user.

With the day's work finally apportioned between them, and after hearing each of the other members' own reports, they hurried to their respective offices.

That is, everyone except Laetitia, who remained where she was, glaring at Ernest.

"Come now, why are you making such a face, Laetitia?"

"Don't play dumb," she said brusquely. "You were going to tell me about the Inquisitors."

Was I, now? Ernest wondered, before folding his hands behind his head and sinking deep into thought. Realizing that there was probably no getting out of it, he decided, albeit reluctantly, to confide in her: "You're the person I least wanted to tell, but all right… It looks like Galaxy is making their play. It's been confirmed by Sinodomius's highest sources."

"They are…?"

"Yes. Their operations unit seems to have already entered the city."

At this, Laetitia's expression turned pale. "They wouldn't…!"

"Judging by the situation, it looks like they would. Their target is undoubtedly Miss Enfield."

"But *now*, after all that…?" Laetitia's voice trembled in disbelief.

Ernest could understand her shock.

He didn't know precisely why, but it was clear that Claudia was trying to antagonize Galaxy. Whatever the issue was, it had to have something to do with that professor she had mentioned during her interview several days prior, Ladislav Bartošik with the Jade Twilight Incident.

But Ernest hadn't expected Galaxy to resort to such measures over that. They obviously didn't want Ladislav's relationship with them to become common knowledge, but even so, all that was in the past now. On the contrary, dealing with Claudia in such an extreme fashion, just when the other five integrated enterprise foundations had begun to be extra vigilant toward them, was all but guaranteed to act against their interests.

If they were to delay things, even just for a little while, they would be able to deal with her quietly, without exacerbating the matter. And yet, they had chosen such a drastic approach.

Ernest sat with his hands folded, deep in thought. *Perhaps she knows more than she's letting on...? Something that Galaxy can't afford to overlook...?*

In any event, now that it had come to this, it could be assumed that Gallardworth's parent organization, the IEF Elliott-Pound, would be watching carefully. With Galaxy moving against the leader of their own academy's star team right in the middle of the Gryps, Elliott-Pound would be observing them with the highest vigilance. The same would apply, no doubt, to the other foundations, too.

Eliminating Claudia was a sudden change in policy, considering how much effort Galaxy had put into protecting her up till now, but it was the most plausible theory.

Even putting the Gryps aside, if Galaxy was to carry out such a plot, that would still provide their competitors with other opportunities to take advantage of. After all, the assassination of the student council president of one's own school right in the middle of the Festa was unprecedented. Of course, they wouldn't be so sloppy as to leave any obvious evidence leading back to them, but they wouldn't be able to completely conceal what had happened, either, and that alone would be enough for the other foundations to act upon. It would be a particularly advantageous card to hold against Galaxy should anything pop up in the future.

And if, by chance, Claudia was to survive, and go on to win the Festa, and meet with Ladislav as per her wish, that, too, would likely reveal new weaknesses that could be manipulated in turn.

No matter how one looked at it, as far as the other foundations were concerned, the best thing to do would be to wait it out and do nothing.

However—

"I... I won't let them...!" Laetitia piped up, her fists clenched. She was biting her lip so hard that she looked as if she might draw blood.

She pulled her mobile out of her pocket, her trembling fingers initiating a call.

"...Agh! Why won't it connect?!"

She must have tried to contact Claudia, but the call hadn't gone through. *Or perhaps*, Ernest wondered, *Claudia was no longer able to answer.*

"It's highly likely that Sinodomius will have taken note of that. If you're going to contact her, you need to do so properly and refrain from doing anything that might compromise you both."

"Ugh...!" Laetitia fretted, chewing her nails in worry.

Her eyes were burning with anger, but Ernest couldn't tell whether it was directed at Galaxy or Claudia.

Or perhaps both of them.

"Is that righteous indignation at Galaxy's disreputable course of action, Laetitia?" Ernest pressed. "Or is it due to your own prideful quest for revenge?"

"Th-that's...," Laetitia stammered.

He didn't know exactly what kind of relationship the two had, but it was clear enough that, for Laetitia, Claudia occupied a very special place in her heart.

Laetitia didn't seem willing to disclose it, however.

"Very well. I will try to look into this myself, as well."

"Huh?" Laetitia looked up at him in surprise. "B-but if you do that, given your position..."

Laetitia seemed to have already understood that Elliott-Pound would adopt a wait-and-see attitude. As the student council president, Ernest was, of course, unable to act against the interests of the school's parent organization. If he did and was found out, he would be unable to avoid disciplinary action.

And yet—

"He who holds the title of Pendragon cannot turn a blind eye to a lady in need. Of course, that goes for my personal feelings, too."

"...Do you have a plan?"

"I'm afraid that, just like you said, my position doesn't afford me many options."

Laetitia pursed her lips in annoyance. "What on earth are you saying?"

"Now, now, let me finish. I might not have a plan or any real options, but I do have an idea."

"Go on."

"I'll need someone else to make the first move."

Laetitia cocked her head to one side.

She didn't appear to have made the connection.

"You've been dying to have a rematch against Miss Enfield, but there's someone else who has also been looking forward to a match against her team, isn't there, now?"

"Ah...!" As he had expected, that hint had been enough for her to connect the dots. "R-right, she might just be willing to ignore the foundations... But are you sure she'll do what you're thinking?"

"Come now, I myself offered her no small amount of assistance during the school fair. It's about time she returned the favor. I'm sure she'll have no complaints," he said with a light smile as he reached for the device on his desk. "And besides, if I use the hotline, not even Sinodomius will have an easy time listening in."

*

"Oh-ho, so you want to use *me*, do you? You've more gall than I thought, Pendragon." Xinglou Fan let out a dry laugh as she gazed at the handsome face projected in the air-window.

"My apologies if I offended you, princess."

In the audience chamber of Jie Long Seventh Institute's Hall of the Yellow Dragon, Xinglou, having just finished her morning training, was sitting on a chair that was unnaturally large, especially in proportion to her small body.

Hufeng, crouching down beside her with a hand on his knee, found himself praying that his impulsive and uninhibited master wouldn't stick her nose into something that didn't concern them.

"I certainly do owe you for the Gran Colosseo... But don't you think this goes a little beyond that?" Xinglou replied.

Hufeng nodded strongly in agreement.

"Do you think so?" the voice on the other end of the call asked. *"The*

way I see it, Miss Lyyneheym only agreed to participate because she knew I had already done so. You might say that it was thanks to me that you had two top-ranked fighters to evaluate your guardians against."

"...Hmm, you do have a point."

Hufeng shook his head in disagreement.

"*But I do understand that I'm asking a lot,*" the caller went on. "*So what do you say about this, princess? I would be willing to invite you to our next official ranking matches—as a spectator, of course.*"

"Oh-ho!"

This is bad, Hufeng thought. That was precisely the kind of lure that Xinglou would snap up in a heartbeat.

Official ranking matches, being key elements of each school's publicity campaigns, were normally held in the city's various public arenas. Matches between unnamed students, however, tended to take place within the grounds of each school, and so, unless they were broadcast, they could only be watched by students from that school. As such, schools sometimes liked to hide a secret ace away from prying eyes in preparation for the Festa. Xinglou herself was, of course, also involved in such activities.

Moreover, it wasn't the battles between unnamed students themselves that formed the main attraction of such matches, but rather the fact that they were the perfect place to discover yet unseen talent. Among the Festa's most die-hard fans, there were those who placed special weight on such matches.

Hufeng could sense a bad feeling welling up inside him.

"*And above all, princess, aren't you looking forward to watching the battle between your favorite pupils and Team Enfield? At this rate, they're on track to lose the most vital component of their fighting potential. Normally, that might be something to rejoice about, but not for you, am I right in assuming?*" Ernest, it seemed, knew precisely how to close the deal.

"Hmm... The Pan-Dora's girl certainly is the heart of the team. It *would* spoil the fun to take her out of the picture..."

"*As you know, Sinodomius is under the jurisdiction of my academy's integrated enterprise foundation, so I'm very limited in how I can react to this. Jie Long's Gaishi, however, is under your direct control. There must be something that you would be able to do about this matter, princess?"*

The intelligence organizations belonging to each of Asterisk's six schools differed in their strengths and structures, but as a general rule, they each operated under the management of their schools' IEF. Even if the student councils of each school were permitted to make use of their services, that right was only given to them on a provisional basis by their respective overlord, so it was always clear who they truly served.

That said, the situation was slightly different for Jie Long and Allekant.

Allekant, for example, took factionalism to an extreme, so much so that each individual faction employed its own independent intelligence agents.

Jie Long's intelligence organization, Gaishi, on the other hand, had been personally established by the first Ban'yuu Tenra, and since then had historically been attached to the student council directly, with only tenuous links to their enterprise foundation.

"Moreover, enticements aside, if I'm not mistaken, princess, you aren't the kind of person who likes to watch on in silence, are you?"

"Hmm, are you trying to fan the flames, boy? Don't get too full of yourself." For a brief second, there was something dangerous about her tone, although it quickly disappeared. "But very well. Consider me intrigued."

Upon hearing this response, Hufeng lifted his hands to his head.

Somehow, he had suspected from the beginning that things might end up like this, but that was precisely why he wouldn't allow himself to nod along to everything meekly.

"...With all due respect, Master, I don't think it would be wise to involve ourselves with another school's troubles at this time."

"Don't say that, Hufeng. You'll be upset, too, if your opponents can't fight at their full strength."

"That may be so, but still..."

Team Enfield would be Hufeng's—Team Yellow Dragon's—next

opponent. As a martial artist, it was, of course, natural that he would prefer to fight them at their best.

However, that was a separate matter entirely. He couldn't stay silent when another school was trying to induce them into engaging in unnecessary risks.

"A-anyway, you should at least think about it before—"

"No. I've decided," Xinglou said with an innocent smile, prior to sounding a small, clear bell.

Hearing that sound, Hufeng let out a tired sigh. He really was at his wits' end.

There was no turning back now.

Because before the sound could even fade back into silence, *she* appeared in front of them.

"Hiya! Did you call me, little Xinglou?"

Appearing as if out of thin air was a young woman. Much to Hufeng's chagrin, he was still unable to sense her presence.

She had large catlike eyes, cropped unruly hair, and a short body blessed with a bounty of feminine curves. What was most distinctive of all, however, were the myriad of scars that crisscrossed her entire body, face included, all of which she wore like trophies.

With modern medicine, removing scars was a trivial procedure. In other words, the girl—Alema Seiyng, an operative from the seventh office of the Ryuusei Kyuushi, Jie Long's student council–operated intelligence organization, and renowned for her vicious nature—had decided to keep the scars on purpose.

"Yes, yes. I need to ask you a favor, Alema."

"Well, if it's a job, it's not like I can say no or anything."

Alema didn't speak, per se, but rather, she communicated through text displayed on an air-window floating by her side. The long, collar-like spell charm wrapped around her neck served to seal her voice away.

"*Ah, Seiten Taisei. I don't believe we've seen each other since the closing ceremony of the Phoenix*," Ernest said in greeting.

"Oh, if it isn't little Ernest. Long time no see," Alema replied with a vacant smile, waving back at him.

The two were acquaintances of a sort. Alema, being Xinglou's favorite, was often sent to represent her in her stead whenever she was absent from official engagements.

"Hee-hee! I saw you in the Gryps. You look good. Why don't you have a go with me next time?"

"*That's impossible!*" Laetitia broke in, forcing her way into the frame of the air-window. *"I've told you again and again, duels aren't allowed here at Gallardworth! As the student council president, he of all people can't break the rules! And why are you acting so chummy with him anyway?!"*

"Eh, no fun." Alema pouted in disappointment.

Hufeng, however, had nodded along with Laetitia in agreement. He had found himself obliged on occasion to take issue with Alema's rough-spoken and overly familiar attitude with Xinglou. That said, she wasn't the kind of person to pay much heed to what others had to say, and Xinglou, it seemed, was more than happy to allow her to keep acting that way.

Alema Seiyng, also known as the Sage of Heavenly Enlightenment, Seiten Taisei, was Jie Long's former number one—meaning, she had been Jie Long's strongest fighter up until Xinglou had taken her place.

Xinglou had invited the defeated Alema to become one of her disciples, but the scarred girl had turned her down. Xinglou, however, valuing her talents, still wanted to make her her own, and so she had offered her a compromise.

In short, she became not a disciple, but a member of Gaishi, and in exchange, she had the right to challenge Xinglou to a duel whenever she wished. Being just as much a fanatic for battle as Xinglou, Alema had agreed to this readily, and even now, she challenged her at every possible opportunity.

"So the job?"

"First things first, Alema. Are you aware that Galaxy brought some people here to Rikka yesterday?"

"Huh? Nope, no idea what you're talking about." She shook her head, expression vacant.

"Gallardworth's Sinodomius noticed them. I guess our people must be taking it pretty easy, huh?" Hufeng said, his voice practically dripping with sarcasm.

Alema merely scratched at the back of her head, without showing even the slightest embarrassment. "Their information network is on a completely different scale than ours. There's no need to compare."

"Yes, that's fine. More importantly, I don't feel like letting them have what they want. That's your job," Xinglou said, a piercing glint flashing in her eyes.

"Hmm... Got it. So Galaxy's people. Who are they, exactly?"

"According to Pendragon, it sounds like Night Emit. Their head seems to be with them, too."

"Oh, this'll be good! The head of the Yabuki is supposed to be pretty strong, right? I'm getting revved up!" Alema punched a fist into her free hand, flashing them all a brutal grin.

The flames burning in her eyes were just like Xinglou's when she got worked up.

"Unfortunately, I don't know how strong the current head is, although I do remember facing one of their previous ones a few generations back. He..." Xinglou tilted her head to one side, as if trying to recall something, before clapping her hands together in excitement. "That's it. He put up quite the fight, if I remember correctly. Yes, he really had me on the back foot there. Good memories."

"What?! Ah, I'm looking forward to this now!"

"Let me say this. Their techniques are truly troublesome. You would be wise not to take on their head, in particular."

"And why wouldn't I?" Alema retorted, her grin growing yet more fiendish.

"...Well, so long as you take care of the job, I don't really mind."

Listening to this back and forth, Hufeng broke into a frown, his headache only growing stronger.

Why was it that only these kinds of people tended to flock to Xinglou?

"...Then it sounds like the matter is settled. Well then, princess, shall I leave it to you for now?" Ernest asked with an uncertain smile.

"Very well. And what do you intend to do?"

"Of course, we'll do everything we can from our side, too... But if we were able to handle it alone, I wouldn't have needed to call you. Isn't that right, Laetitia?" Ernest glanced away from the air-window for a brief moment, turning to his side, as if reminding her of something.

So, Hufeng wondered, *Gallardworth must have its fair share of impulsive people, too.*

"Oh-ho, I see. That's true."

"Well then, we're counting on you, princess."

And with that, the air-window snapped shut.

"I'D BETTER GO GET READY, THEN," Alema murmured, before disappearing just as suddenly as she had appeared.

Though he stretched his senses as much as he could, Hufeng still hadn't been able to detect her leaving. Grinding his teeth in annoyance, he turned toward his leader. "Are you sure about this, Master? Making trouble with an integrated enterprise foundation now would be..."

"Fret not. So long as the Ban'yuu Tenra is involved, they won't dare make a move against us. Anyway, the Gryps this time has been rather dreary, wouldn't you say? Perhaps this will add a little spice to things?" she said with an innocent laugh.

Hufeng let out a heavy sigh. The reason that such people flocked to Xinglou was no doubt because she herself could be just as reckless as they were.

CHAPTER 3
MEMORIES III: MORNING

"Y-y-you confessed...?!" While Julis tried to maintain her composure, she couldn't stop her voice from coming out as a nervous stammer.

"Yes." Saya nodded calmly.

They were in their training room, just before noon.

Julis and Kirin opened their eyes wide in shock.

"H-hold on, Saya. Does that, I mean, did you...? You mean, you told Ayato...about how you feel?" Julis asked again, to make sure she hadn't misunderstood.

But Saya's answer remained unchanged. "That's what I'm saying."

"O-oh, I see, that's..."

It looked to be true. No sooner did Julis realize that than an indescribable wave of uneasiness welled up in her chest.

"But I mean, that's... That's..."

She had so many things she wanted to ask her, but she didn't know how to put them into words.

It would, after all, be a confession of her own.

But more than that, this was a confession from Saya, Ayato's childhood companion, that she was facing; the person who, though they had been separated for many years, had been his closest and most familiar friend.

Thinking about it as an outsider, even if Saya had merely expressed her honest feelings, the fact that she, who should have wanted above

KOKURI
(NOD)

all else merely to maintain her past relationship with Ayato, had instead taken this step, suggested that it wouldn't perhaps be out of the question to believe that Ayato felt something similar.

And if that was true, there was every possibility he would accept her confession, in which case—

Julis, having started going down this train of thought, found her eyes spinning around in alarm and put her head in her hands.

"U-um! A-Ayato's response—wh-what did he say...?!" Kirin, who had remained completely petrified up till now, broke in feverishly, looking as if she might start crying at any moment.

Right, that's it!

Julis snapped back to her senses and gave a hearty nod at hearing Kirin ask the very question that should have been on the tip of her own tongue.

But when she looked carefully at the younger girl, she could see that Kirin's eyes were darting in every direction, just like her own had been. She was clearly at her limit.

Moreover, her legs were shaking terribly, as if they might give way at any moment, and her whole body was trembling like a small, terrified animal's. She seemed to be taking it much worse than Julis.

"He didn't give me an answer."

"Huh...?" Julis and Kirin asked in confusion.

"I said he could tell me later. I only wanted to tell him how I felt," Saya answered plainly.

Julis let out a sigh of relief, but then she immediately rebuked herself.

Why should I be so happy about that...?

Lately, Julis's emotions seemed to be getting thrown into disorder on a regular basis, like when Ayato had gone to the school fair with Sylvia. It wasn't a good feeling.

It's none of my business who he decides to hang around with... Although he is a teammate, so I guess I could say something... Anyway, he's free to do what he wants, and I've got no right to... No, he did say to my face that he wanted to be my strength, so maybe I should... No, no, I can't complain, but I... Argh!

Once again, her train of thought had begun to take her somewhere it shouldn't, but she managed to bring herself back to her senses before it could go too far. She swung her head back and forth as if to shake free from it all.

"Whew..." Kirin slumped to the floor. She, too, seemed to have lost all energy. "B-but why are you telling us...?" she asked.

"I just want to play fair with my rivals... Good luck, you two," Saya said without any hesitation.

Kirin jumped to her feet. "Th-that's, I mean, I— I'm not...!"

"R-right! Wh-what are you talking about?!" Julis found herself exclaiming, a rush of blood coming to her cheeks.

"If that's the case, then fine. Whatever you do, just don't regret it afterward." Saya nodded expressionlessly.

"Um..."

"Argh..."

Saya's words seemed to weigh heavily on them both.

N-no, I can't, I can't. Calm down...

Julis's rhythm had been disturbed for a while now.

She took a deep breath to calm her nerves, before turning to Saya. "W-well, I mean, I'm not trying to pry or anything, but more importantly, why did you have to do it right in the middle of the Gryps? I mean, all it would take is one wrong move to sow trouble in the team... N-not that we're upset or anything, but you know."

"Yes... Sorry." And with that, Saya bowed her head to her two teammates. "The timing was due to my own selfishness. I'm sorry." At that point, she raised her head to stare straight into Julis's eyes. "Maybe this goes without saying, but I don't think that any of us would let our feelings get in the way of the tournament. So I thought it would be okay."

"That's..." Julis, finding herself in complete agreement with her logic, was at a loss for words.

She was confident that both she and Kirin had the strength of mind to concentrate fully on their upcoming matches without distraction.

Both, she was sure, were able to distinguish between the two issues and deal with each separately. Moreover, both she and Kirin had their own reasons for wanting to win at the Festa, reasons that they wouldn't let anything get in the way of.

And she knew, as well, that Saya had no such motivation.

Saya was fighting for Ayato. That was no doubt why she was able to bring herself to confess her feelings to him without worrying that any of the others would hold it against her.

"But Enfield is different," Saya added. "I'm a little concerned about her."

"Huh…? The president?" Kirin's eyes flickered with uncertainty.

Julis, however, had wondered the same thing. "There's no need to worry about her, I think. She might act that way, but there's no one better than her at looking at things rationally."

There was no mistaking that Claudia was particularly assertive with Ayato, and Julis couldn't deny that she had her concerns about that, but as to whether or not she was seriously looking for that kind of relationship with him, she had no idea whatsoever.

Kirin nodded in agreement, but Saya, in contrast, slowly shook her head.

"I don't think so. I knew it as soon as I saw her. She's serious."

"…Oh? What makes you think that?"

"Just my intuition."

Saya's answer was incredibly straightforward, but Julis knew better than to take it lightly. "Hmm…"

At that moment, however, the training room doors slid open, and Ayato, dressed in his workout clothes, his forehead beaded with sweat, strode in.

"Sorry. Am I late…? I was doing some solo conditioning and lost track of time."

His breathing was rough, meaning he had probably run all the way to the training room.

"Good morning, Ayato," Saya beamed, running up to greet him.

"…! …Ah, Saya. Good morning," Ayato replied with the same gentle greeting as usual.

Julis, however, couldn't fail to take note of a brief flash of nervousness darting through his eyes.

"It's okay—we're not all here yet," Saya said. "Here, Ayato." She handed him a towel.

Perhaps it was just her imagination, but Julis couldn't help thinking Saya was acting more intimately with Ayato than normal. They might have been childhood friends, so close as to be almost family, but there seemed to be something different in the way she was acting.

"...Right, thanks." Ayato, on the other hand, seemed only a little awkward as he accepted the towel.

He was probably conscious of Saya's change in behavior as well. It was clear that their relationship wasn't moving in a bad direction.

"Uh, I'll get it back to you once I've washed it..."

"It's okay. Don't worry about it."

"I'll wash it."

"...I said it's okay." Saya pouted, trying to wrest it from him, her body coming awfully close to his.

"Ah..." Saya, seemingly having realized the situation, suddenly pulled away from him. Her expression remained unchanged, but she cast her eyes to the ground, her cheeks turning slightly pink.

That was not the kind of reaction she would have had in the past.

Julis and Kirin watched on from a distance.

"...Wh-what is it, Kirin?" Saya asked, turning toward her. "If you want to ask Ayato something, just say it."

"What?! I—I—I don't..." Kirin shrank with fear, her eyes brimming with tears, before she turned toward Julis. "J-Julis, um, d-do you...?"

"M-me?! Ah, right, um... N-no, nothing!"

"Oh... I—I see... Sorry..."

"I-I'm not angry or anything, look," Julis said hastily, trying to console her. She let out a deep breath in an attempt to calm her nerves, though it didn't do much good. "...She does have courage, though. We ought to applaud her for that."

"...Yes."

What she was aiming for was different, but Julis knew all too well how terrifying it could be to take the first step toward bringing about change.

Saya's determination was worthy of respect.

"You said we're not all here yet... But it's already time, right?" Ayato asked, checking his mobile and glancing around the training room.

They were supposed to be having a strategy meeting to discuss tomorrow's semifinal match. Their opponents, Team Yellow Dragon, would easily be the strongest team they had faced thus far.

Xiaohui Wu, alias the Celestial Warrior, Hagun Seikun, would be particularly difficult. His martial art abilities would make defeat all but inevitable without an adequate counterstrategy. All his skills, in particular his spearmanship and *seisenjutsu*, that he had demonstrated in the second round were alarming in and of themselves, but taken as a whole, they made him truly terrifying.

"Right, the president isn't here yet...," Kirin said.

"She isn't normally late," Julis observed.

In fact, as far as Julis could remember, Claudia had never been late to a meeting.

"Ah, looks like I've got a call. Maybe it's... Huh?" She broke into a frown. The number on her mobile was unregistered.

She couldn't help but feel a wave of uncertainty as she opened a blacked-out air-window.

It was a voice-only call.

"...! Ah! Thank God! You picked up!"

There was a lot of distortion and noise, but Julis recognized the voice.

"...Laetitia?"

They might have been acquaintances, of a sort, but they certainly weren't close enough to call each other directly.

"Yes, it's me. We don't have much time, so let me get right to the point. Is Claudia there?"

"What's this about...? Anyway, she isn't here yet."

"No, it can't be...!" The voice on the other side of the air-window was filled with despair.

"What's going on? If you've got something to say to Claudia, why don't you just call her yourself?"

"I'm calling you because I can't *reach her! Anyway, you need to go look for her now and make sure she's safe!"*

"Safe…? Wait, what does that mean?! What are you talking about?!" Julis could tell from the urgency in Laetitia's voice that whatever it was, it was no trivial matter.

Ayato, Kirin, and Saya, listening on beside her in silence, were each wearing serious expressions.

"We don't have time! I've only got another thirty seconds before Sinodomius traces this line! Galaxy is making their move!"

That was enough for them to understand the gravity of the situation. "Got it. I don't know the details, but thanks."

"One more thing—I need to talk to Ayato Amagiri!"

"To Ayato…?" Julis repeated, glancing toward him.

Ayato stepped forward with a slight nod. "What's wrong?"

"It's—"

*

It had been some time since Claudia had gone to watch the Lindvolus.

"Claudia. I have a present for you," Isabella said as she offered her a large case.

Claudia glanced toward it in surprise. She couldn't remember her mother ever having given her a present before.

Even as a child, she had had access to practically inexhaustible wealth, and so whatever she wanted, she had it bought for her. It was far different than the act of gift giving.

"To what do I owe this surprise?" she asked with an artificial smile.

"Your birthday is coming up soon, right?" Isabella answered gently.

"That may be so, but still…"

"Come now, have a look," Isabella said to her perplexed daughter, before putting the case on the drawing room table and releasing the lock.

"That's…" Claudia caught her breath as she saw what lay inside.

"Indeed. The Pan-Dora."

An Orga Lux, like a pair of unborn children in deep sleep. Staring at their activators before her, she felt a shudder run through her body, just as she had felt during the Lindvolus.

Watching Claudia rise up from her chair and pull away, Isabella narrowed her eyes in a sweet smile. "Dear me, Claudia. What is it?"

"...Nothing."

"Is it what you felt during the Lindvolus? Excellent. That means it has chosen you as its user." Isabella spread her hands wide as if to indicate that it was a wonderful turn of events.

Claudia caught her breath, trying to pull herself together. "But how were you able to remove an Orga Lux? I thought they were dealt with rather strictly..."

Even if her mother was an executive at its IEF, taking one of the school's Orga Luxes to give to her own daughter seemed like it would fall foul of far too many regulations.

"Heh-heh. Just who do you think I am?" Isabella asked with a laugh. "As it happens, after what occurred during the Lindvolus, the Pan-Dora was to be sealed away. As such, once it had arrived at Galaxy's research facilities, I explained the situation, and they allowed me to borrow it. Our researchers are hoping to garner more data from it themselves, so they were more than happy to oblige."

"It's an honor to be given such a dangerous item," Claudia said, her voice dripping with sarcasm.

Isabella's, however, remained unwavering. "Of course, if you don't want it, I'll take it back. There's no need to force yourself. But just so you know, it's quite rare to be chosen by an Orga Lux, and as far as abilities go, this one is particularly powerful. I thought, perhaps, that it might one day be of some use to you..."

"..."

Isabella might have been her mother, but Claudia found her remarkably difficult to read.

Looking at it analytically, she seemed to want to use her daughter to gather data on the Pan-Dora, which had remarkably few compatible users. That would certainly be of use to Seidoukan Academy, under Galaxy's management.

And yet, it would be of little use to Galaxy itself, and it didn't make much sense for someone with her mother's position to take any special interest in it.

In that case, was it simply a present for her daughter, as she claimed? If it truly did confer upon its user the power of precognition, it would be an Orga Lux beyond compare, so much so that it might even serve to give Claudia, who had yet to decide which path to take in life, some direction.

However, just as Claudia had remarked, it was also an incredibly dangerous item, and almost certainly an unsuitable present to give to one's daughter. Yet, Isabella might have judged her mature and wise enough to handle it. She had to admit, her achievements certainly might warrant such an assessment.

...Maybe it's all those reasons combined.

Her thoughts having taken her this far, she made her decision.

Whether it had to do with people or objects, whenever something happened, it tended to be due to multiple competing forces. All the more so for people like Isabella.

Which was why Claudia chose to accept it for the simplest of reasons—because she was happy to receive a present from her mother.

"I understand. I'll gratefully accept it."

"Very good. I'm so happy to hear that." Isabella laughed, before clapping her hands together and calling the servant, as if suddenly remembering something. "Speaking of which, another present has arrived for you as well."

"Another one?"

Judging by the way she had said it, it didn't sound like it was from her.

Claudia opened the box the servant brought in and discovered a stuffed toy bear around five inches tall, along with a small card.

"My, it's so cute."

"...Who is it from?"

Both the fabric and the stitching were of the finest quality—perfectly matching her tastes—so it only took a glance to realize it was a high-quality item.

She opened the card, completely in the dark as to who could have sent it, only to find an unexpected name written inside.

"Laetitia...?"

"Ah, that young lady from the Blanchard family?" Isabella nodded. "You two get along quite well, don't you?"

"Not particularly..."

The card contained a message: *I'll defeat you next time, so be ready.*

"But you should make sure your father doesn't see it."

"...Yes."

The Enfield family and Blanchard family had seemed to be joined by fate for several hundred years now, ever since the War of the Grand Alliance, and Nicholas, as a direct descendant of the Enfield line, had an innate prejudice against the Blanchards.

And yet, while Claudia wasn't particularly fond of stuffed toys, she couldn't bring herself to throw away a present that someone had gone to all the trouble to give her.

"I'll have to give her something in return. Her birthday was in... February, wasn't it?"

Given that it was June now, there was still quite a while to go.

"In that case, the Opernball in Vienna is around that time. How about you give it to her then?"

The Opernball had been a treasured tradition of the upper classes for centuries, but it had changed in nature somewhat during the Reconstruction following the Invertia. Perhaps most notably, the age of debutantes had been greatly reduced, no doubt so that the European noble houses could search for suitable partners of superior blood at a younger age.

Today, even the great houses couldn't survive without associating with the IEFs. As such, bringing people with outstanding abilities into one's family was simply a matter of necessity.

"...Well, it isn't for a while, so I suppose I have time to find something suitable for her," she murmured, glancing back and forth between the stuffed toy and the Pan-Dora. She found herself unable to hold back a smile at just how surreal the difference between the two was.

* * *

Her choice to accept the Pan-Dora, however, would end up changing her life completely.

"Aaaaaaaaaaaaaaaaaaaaaah!"

The next morning, before the sun had even completely risen, a shrill cry echoed throughout the mansion.

The servants rushed into her room, only to find Claudia breathing raggedly, her eyes wide open, her fingers gripping the edge of her bedsheets so tightly that they had turned a pallid white.

The dream was already vanishing like fog in the morning, fading away into oblivion.

Claudia had tasted the cost demanded by the Pan-Dora, the unendurable suffering and overwhelming fear of experiencing one's own death. The shock was enough to shatter her naive indifference and bring her precocious and slanted sense of self crashing down.

"Oh dear… It looks like it *is* intense." Isabella, having appeared beside her almost instantaneously, looked down at her daughter with pity.

Claudia, her mother's figure in the center of her vision, tried desperately to bring her breathing under control.

"Well then, Claudia, do you still want to hold on to the Pan-Dora?" she asked. Her mother spoke as if she knew this would happen, and yet, there was a touch of disappointment in her voice.

Claudia, however, weakly shook her head.

"Oh?" Isabella raised an eyebrow, as though slightly surprised.

That decision, too, had been for the simplest of reasons—because she refused to give in.

She herself was startled to find that she harbored such childish feelings.

Mustering her strength, she sat up in her bed. "…It was a present. I'll hold on to it for a while longer," she said.

Claudia had managed to maintain that mind-set for close to a month.

When one considered that the Pan-Dora's previous users hadn't even been able to hold out for three days, her tenacity pointed to an astounding strength of will.

The nightmares, however, had continued mercilessly, night after night, without end, eating away at her heart, steadily breaking her spirit.

Then, one night, when she could no longer clearly distinguish between the waking world and her nightmares, and she had begun to feel as if she was reaching her limit...

It was then that she met Ayato for the first time.

*

"Claudia! Are you in there, Claudia?!" Julis called out, banging against her door.

There was no response.

They had wasted no time after speaking to Laetitia, heading straight for Claudia's room in Seidoukan Academy's girls' dormitory.

The door, however, was locked, and with no indication that Claudia was inside, Julis found herself grinding her teeth in worry.

"Damn it! How could I have been so careless?"

She hadn't expected Galaxy to act so soon.

Or rather, she hadn't given Claudia's warning the weight it had deserved.

Making an enemy of Galaxy... When Claudia had told them that that would be the likely outcome of her actions, Julis had prepared herself for the worst, but things had been uneventful since the opening of the Gryps, with everything moving along smoothly.

It wasn't as if she had let down her guard, but she couldn't deny that she had spent her time focusing on the matches in front of her, rather than considering what Galaxy might do next.

It was all due to Claudia's strategizing, and yet, Galaxy, it seemed, hadn't relaxed its efforts to stop her.

"...Julis, step out of the way," Saya said, activating one of her huge Luxes.

"Wha—?! W-wait, Saya! You can't use that in here...!" Kirin, alarmed, tried to talk her out of it.

Julis, however, found herself in agreement with Saya for once. "Do it!"

"*...Boom.*"

A blinding projectile burst out from the weapon with a roar, blasting the door out of its frame.

Other students began to come out into the corridor from the nearby rooms to see what was going on, but Julis paid them no heed, barging inside the room.

"What happened here...?"

Julis glanced around, taken aback by the disastrous scene that lay before her. Inside Claudia's quarters, everything, living room and bedroom alike, appeared to have been completely ransacked.

For a brief instant, she wondered whether it was due to Saya's attack on the door, but the damage was far too extensive for that. The sofa lay on its side, the bedsheets torn into shreds, the walls and carpet damaged and broken almost everywhere.

And on top of that...

"...There's been a fight here, with weapons," Kirin said sternly as she examined the floor. "I can't make out any footprints, but there must have been a lot of people... And there's a bloodstain here."

"*Ngh...!*" Julis bit her lip in concern.

Saya tapped her on the shoulder. "It might not belong to Enfield. She could have struck back at her attackers."

"Maybe..."

But if that was so, why was Claudia missing?

"There isn't a lot of blood, though. And...I think the president must have escaped, once they came for her," Kirin, still investigating the floor, said gravely.

"What makes you say that?"

"It's only a guess...but if Galaxy's people had succeeded, they wouldn't have left the room like this. They might have free rein to do what they want here in Seidoukan, but at the very least, they would try to cover it up. But here..."

Perhaps it was because her uncle worked at Galaxy, but Kirin had an unexpectedly well-informed idea of how the integrated enterprise foundation did things.

"Right! So they mustn't have had time to clean up after themselves..."

"...I see." Saya nodded in understanding.

Whether it was due to a lack of personnel or time, the fact that they had left the room in this state suggested they had something more important to see to.

"That means...," Kirin began, turning toward the window.

The glass was broken, but the shards lay scattered across the balcony, not inside the room.

Julis rushed toward it, and sure enough, there were drops of blood on the balcony as well.

"She must have gone this way..."

Saya pulled at her sleeve, scowling at the destruction. "...We need to tell Ayato."

"Right. He might have found something, too," Julis agreed, reaching for her mobile. She hoped that Claudia was safe, wherever she might be.

CHAPTER 4
MIDDAY

"...You're saying that the Nights are making a move?"

"I guess Galaxy finally ran out of patience."

"Hmph. It's none of *my* business," Dirk Eberwein spat, reclining in his chair in the Le Wolfe Black Institute's student council room, his usual frown carving deep wrinkles across his forehead.

"*Dear me...*," Madiath Mesa, on the other side of the air-window, said with an affected shrug.

"If they do manage to get rid of her, it'll make Seidoukan a hell of a lot easier to deal with. I can't see them finding a replacement like her any time soon."

"*I see. So even you value her abilities, in your own way,*" he joked.

Dirk glared into the air-window. "If that's all you wanted to talk about, I'm hanging up. I'm afraid I don't have as much free time on my hands as you do."

"*Now, now, hold on a minute. You're as hot-headed as always, I see,*" Madiath said, trying to soothe him. "*No, the real issue is this: I only heard it a short while ago. It seems that our Miss Enfield knows about Varda.*"

"What...?" Upon hearing this, even Dirk's face paled in color.

Both Dirk and Madiath were members of a select group known as the Golden Bough Alliance, which, along with certain high-ranking executives in Galaxy, were supposed to be the only people with knowledge of the greatest secrets, including the existence of the only Orga Lux capable of acting independently, based on its own will—the Varda-Vaos.

Everyone else who knew about it had either been quietly taken care of, or else they had their memories erased by the Orga Lux itself, the primary ability of which was mind control.

"She must have brought it up either to try negotiating with Galaxy or else to threaten them. Something like that anyway."

"She's out of her mind."

Trying to do something like that with an integrated enterprise foundation was practically the very definition of suicide.

"Indeed, that's what I'm worried about. Do you really think that someone whose abilities you respect so much would have made such a foolish mistake?"

"...What do you mean?"

"What I'm saying is that everything that's happened so far might all have been as she intended." Madiath paused for a second. *"Think about it. Galaxy brought in the Nights to deal with a student at their own school. That doesn't make any sense. If they had wanted to do something, they could have punished her under some made-up pretext and dealt with it all internally."*

"So she started it all during the Festa, when Galaxy couldn't afford to do anything half-baked, and even went so far as to give the other foundations an opportunity to hold them back... What a snake."

"Considering the circumstances, the best option for Galaxy would simply be to make her disappear. In other words, assassinate her."

Looking at it that way, there *was* a kind of logic to their actions.

And yet...

"But that still leaves the biggest problem. *Why would she do it?*"

From Claudia's perspective, she was only hemming herself in. There was no logical benefit to be had.

"I'm afraid I don't know the answer to that... But there is one thing I can say for sure."

"Yeah?"

"She's human, just like us. It doesn't matter what her wish is—she's

willing to sacrifice anything in order to fulfill it... Or rather, she doesn't even take those secondary matters into consideration to begin with."

"...Hmph."

"*Don't lump me in with you,*" Dirk wanted to spit back.

"*Well, that's the situation, so we'd better keep an eye on her.*"

"What's the point? She's practically dead already."

Night Emit wasn't only ancient, it was one of the most distinguished groups of its kind in the Far East.

It didn't matter how great Claudia's abilities were—there was no way she would be able to escape.

"*Indeed.*" Madiath laughed. "*And yet, I've got a feeling we shouldn't take that for granted.*" He flashed Dirk a suspicious smile before ending the call.

"..." Dirk, left alone, crossed him arms and sank deep into thought.

Finally, with a click of his tongue, he opened another air-window. "Make sure Korona gets here quickly—*before* evening. And start spreading a rumor—indirectly. Seidoukan's student council president seems to be missing."

*

"...I see. Thanks, Julis. I'll call you later. Make sure you... Right, I'll leave it to you."

Ayato closed the small air-window and let out a tired sigh. "She isn't in her dorm room," he muttered in a low voice. "And according to Julis, it looks like there was a fight of some kind..."

He was sitting alone at a four-person table in the back of a gloomy diner on the outskirts of the commercial area, a cup of mud-like coffee in his hand.

"Just as I thought," a voice from behind him said.

She too had spoken so softly that he could barely make out the words, but the voice belonged to the student council vice president of Saint Gallardworth Academy, Laetitia Blanchard.

Glancing over his shoulder, he watched as the young lady, her elegance quite at odds with the somewhat cheerless diner, lifted her cup of tea to her lips.

There was no denying that she stood out, but there was nothing he could do about that.

"Anyway, I'm surprised you knew this place. It's certainly suitable for off-the-record talks… Although the clientele leaves something to be desired." Laetitia spoke as if she was somehow impressed with the place and yet at the same time taking issue with it.

"No, I only found out about it from someone else…," Ayato explained, looking down into his coffee.

It was the same diner where he had gone with Irene for information on Flora's kidnapping during the last Festa. It was, after all, a rather shady establishment, so it was little wonder that Laetitia found it suspicious.

In other words, it was more suited to students from Le Wolfe than from Gallardworth.

"Well, you're helping me out, so I won't pry. I'm not very familiar with these kinds of places, and yet…"

"…And yet?"

"I'm not impressed that you frequent such a dubious place. I've heard that you often go to the Rotlicht as well. If you're going to be friends with Claudia, you really need to think about improving your character a little."

"I came here for a specific reason last time…," he tried to explain, but Laetitia wouldn't hear it.

"The Enfield family is just as distinguished in Europe as the Blanchard family. If you go around behaving in a way unbecoming of that name, it won't just reflect poorly on you—you'll drag Claudia down as well. And if that happens, I'll never forgive you."

"Right…"

For some reason, Laetitia seemed to be taking offense at all the wrong things.

It was clear, however, from the way she was speaking, that she truly was worried for Claudia.

"Listen up, Ayato Amagiri! If I'm being honest, I still haven't

accepted you. I'm only asking for your help now because I don't have any other options. Keep that in mind!"

"Right… So what did you want to tell me?" he prompted. If he let her keep going on like that, she might never tell him.

"Yes… Ahem. Very well," she said, clearing her throat.

Ayato had only suggested the diner in the first place because she had said that she wanted to speak to him in person.

After all, it sounded like they couldn't afford to talk over the phone.

"I want to find Claudia as quickly as possible as well," he told her.

She seemed to hesitate for the briefest of moments, before answering: "Then you need to hear this. It might prove vital to save her."

In that case, she needed to come out with it, Ayato thought.

"…Just so you know, it was Claudia herself who told me this, and she made me promise not tell anyone else. I always intended to honor that promise, but now… Now I guess I don't have any choice."

"What is it?"

But instead of answering him, Laetitia asked a question of her own: "Before that, do you know what Claudia's wish is—why she came to Asterisk?"

"Well… She wants to meet Ladislav Bartošik, the professor who was involved in the Jade Twilight Incident."

Claudia had said as much during their winners' interview several days ago, so that should have been public knowledge. Ayato personally, however, couldn't help but wonder if her real goal wasn't something else.

"Indeed. I saw her say that during the interview. But you know… That's completely different than what she told me once before."

"What…?"

Ayato was about to turn around, when, perhaps sensing this, Laetitia continued: "Let me start from the beginning. She and I used to be rivals, always competing against each other for victory in tournaments throughout Europe… In the end, I wasn't ever able to beat her, though…"

"Right…"

Laetitia's voice was filled with chagrin, muffled, as if she were biting on a handkerchief.

"Ahem. Anyway, during one tournament, she was in unusually high spirits. And she told me that she had finally found a wish that she wanted to have granted."

"She was in high spirits? Claudia...?" Ayato had only known her for just over a year, but he had yet to see that side of her.

"Yes. I was surprised, too. I asked her to tell me, but she wouldn't say anything more about it. I ended up getting so angry that I made a bet with her that if I won the next match, she would have to tell me everything."

"...But didn't you just say you weren't able to beat her?"

In that case, she must have lost that bet.

Perhaps she had taken offense at those words, as she continued in a serious, quick voice: "R-right, but don't interrupt! She was clearly acting strange during that tournament. I heard afterward that she had just gotten her hands on the Pan-Dora. She couldn't use it because of the tournament's regulations, but still..."

"The Pan-Dora...? Wait, hold on. I thought you said this happened when you were both still kids?"

Orga Luxes were only supposed to be used inside Asterisk. Of course, there were always exceptions, such as when Ayato had gone to Lieseltania, so it wasn't impossible to take them outside the city, given that the user undertook the proper administrative procedures. Moreover, a winner in the Festa might use their wish to take private possession of an Orga Lux, but even in such cases, ownership would only last for the user's lifetime, before reverting to the relevant foundation. Giving one to a child who wasn't even a student at Asterisk, however—that was an extraordinary exception.

"I was surprised to hear it, too... But then, given her mother's position, it probably wasn't all that difficult. Even then, the woman was already close to the top at Galaxy. Moreover, I don't think she had it all the time. They sent it back every now and then for analysis." Laetitia paused there, sipping from her cup of tea. "Anyway, that's how it was. She clearly wasn't in a good way, and the final ended in a draw."

"A draw…?"

"Neither of us won, and neither of us lost. So after making me promise never to tell anyone, she offered to tell me half of her wish," Laetitia said with a small sigh. "Her wish—Claudia's wish—was to dedicate herself fully to her destined partner."

"…Huh?" Ayato inadvertently let that out, taken aback by what he had just heard. "Dedicate herself? To her destined partner?"

He had no idea what kind of person she had been as a child, but that kind of thing certainly didn't match the Claudia he knew.

"Well, I was just as confused when I heard it. At first, I thought she was pulling my leg, so I asked her about this destined partner. And she told me that she hadn't met him yet."

Ayato could understand why she would think Claudia had been joking.

"But then she went to Seidoukan and rose to the position of student council president… And then, watching her actions, it suddenly all made sense to me. That destined partner she was talking about—it has to be you, Ayato Amagiri."

"What?!" he exclaimed, spinning around. Realizing what he had done, he quickly turned back to his own table, lowering his voice: "…How did that happen?"

"To tell you the truth, at first, I thought you must have tricked her, but now…"

"I—I didn't do anything like that…"

"Don't worry. I'm not that bad a judge of character. I can tell from what you've done so far that, if nothing else, you're not a bad person at heart." Despite her words, there did seem to be a touch of displeasure in her voice. "Anyway, she put a huge amount of effort—and not just her own—into finding you and recommending you for a special scholarship. You, with no achievements, nothing at all to your name. That was the only time she had ever done anything like that—so I knew right away, it had to be you."

"…" Ayato remained silent. He, too, had long wondered why the opportunity had come to him of all people.

He had tried to ask her about it the first time they had met. After all, he wasn't the kind of outstanding student who would be considered a candidate for a scholarship—let alone be offered one. Claudia had said there had been a lot of opposition, but she had pushed through with his candidacy regardless. But in that case, how had she known about him to begin with?

"...This is just a guess, but I think she must have seen you in those nightmares that she has from using the Pan-Dora."

"The Pan-Dora...? But I thought her memories of those faded away when she woke up?"

He was sure she had said something like that.

"That does seem to be the case. But she must have said something like this as well, that some fragments and impressions remain. What do you think? Even if they are just fragments, would they really be so strong as to completely change someone's outlook on life?"

In the back of his mind, Ayato remembered something Claudia had said back when they had first met.

"At last... We meet at last."

She had embraced him from behind, in the middle of the student council room.

Thinking back, her actions then had been completely at odds with her usual self. She had spoken with a fragile, helpless voice—a voice that he hadn't heard again since.

"Basically, she must have met you in her dreams and fallen for you... Then she decided to come here, to Asterisk, meet you, and dedicate herself to you. That must have been her wish. To be honest, I think it's a pretty stupid one, but that's a different matter."

Personally, Ayato found it somewhat difficult to accept, but when he looked at it objectively, he couldn't deny that it all made sense.

"But then why does she have to participate in the Festa...?"

If Laetitia's conclusions were true, then there would have been no need for Claudia to fight in the Gryps or make an enemy of Galaxy.

"Exactly!" Laetitia let out enthusiastically, as if she had only been building up to this point. "She only told me half her wish—so the other half has to be related to what's going on now."

"The other half... Do you think it has something to do with Professor Bartošik and the Jade Twilight Incident?"

Ayato couldn't see much of a connection between the two issues.

"That's what I want to ask you... Ayato Amagiri, what do you know about it?"

"...Me?"

But there was no way he could know any more about the incident than she already did.

"I hadn't even heard of the professor until Claudia brought him up," he answered with a shake of his head—though he knew that Laetitia couldn't see it.

"Really? You're not hiding anything?"

"No, I swear."

"Hmm... Fine." Laetitia's voice seemed to be filled with disappointment.

"Anyway, all that aside, you must be one of the most important keys to this mystery. I'm sure of it."

"Well... I guess so."

He didn't feel so sure himself, but based on everything she had said, he couldn't deny the possibility that she might be right.

"So you need to find her and convince her to give up on it. You're the only one who would be able to do it."

"That's...," he began, before falling silent, at a loss for words.

Did he even have the right to make her give up on her wish, he wondered, especially given everything she had done to come this far?

"Even assuming that she manages to pull through this, once the integrated enterprise foundations start to do something, they never give up. You understand that, right? In this world, to oppose the integrated enterprise foundations is basically to sign your own death warrant. No matter what that wish of hers is, it can't be worth more than her life."

It was clear from Laetitia's sincerity that she was truly concerned about her. That was enough for Ayato.

"...All right," he said with a nod.

There probably were *wishes that people would be willing to stake one's life on*, he thought. But even so, he didn't want to lose Claudia over it.

"...In that case, I'll believe in you. Take this."

A small silver charm dropped onto the sofa where Ayato was sitting.

"What is it?"

"Claudia gave it to me as a birthday present a long time ago. It's supposed to *bring good luck*... Although, it was a pretty unpleasant present."

"Unpleasant...?" Ayato had no idea what she was talking about.

"Don't worry about it. Anyway, please give it to her. She can think of it as my revenge, if she wants."

*

Ayato stepped out of the diner into a dark, early fall day.

The sun was hidden behind thick clouds, and the damp wind carried a distinctive aroma. According to the weather forecast, rain was expected later in the evening.

"...Anyway, I need to find Claudia," he muttered to himself as he hurried toward the road leading back to the school.

What could have motivated her to do this? He had no choice but to ask her directly. If, as Laetitia had said, he was one of the keys to the mystery, he had to find her no matter what it took.

Just as he had come to that realization, his mobile began to ring.

He hurriedly opened an air-window, only to be met with an unexpected face.

"Huh? Sylvie?"

"Ayato, I heard what happened. It sounds serious."

"Ah, yeah. It is... But how did you find out about it?"

"I am *a student council president, you know, and here at Queenvale we* do *have our own intelligence organization, Benetnasch. They aren't half bad."*

Just like Laetitia had at Gallardworth, it looked like the other schools were starting to catch on to the situation, if belatedly.

"That's it! Can you use Benetnasch to try to work out where she is right now?" he asked, a glimmer of hope having revealed itself.

Sylvia, however, merely shook her head apologetically. *"I'm sorry, Ayato. They didn't say anything about her current whereabouts, and I doubt they would tell me even if they do know."*

Just as a part of him had expected, the higher-ups at Queenvale also considered the best approach to be to let things play out.

They would, of course, know about Sylvia's friendship with Ayato, and so there was little chance that they would divulge such information to her.

"But you know, I've been thinking about it myself, and—"

But before she could finish speaking, the air-window suddenly went black.

"...Huh? No signal?"

That was not a message he expected to see in the middle of Asterisk. With the exception of certain areas, such as the underground block where Saya had found herself several days ago, there should have been good reception throughout the entire city.

Wondering what was going on, Ayato lifted his gaze to his surroundings and paused in shock. Without him realizing it, the scenery around him had completely changed. The streets were devoid of passersby, and the buildings around him were in a dilapidated state. He was in the redevelopment area.

"How did I...?"

He should have been going in the other direction, back toward Seidoukan, and yet, he had found himself here. Not only that, now that he had stopped in the middle of the street, a thick fog had begun to rise up around him.

It was clearly an atypical mistake.

He put himself on guard, scanning his surroundings, when a ghostlike figure began to emerge from the mist.

"—?!"

"...It's a concealment technique, one that interferes with the target's sense of direction. It's practically impossible to counter if the target doesn't realize what's happened to them."

"Huh? That voice… Yabuki?!"

"Yep, right on the mark."

The figure continued toward him through the fog, until finally Ayato could make out his roommate's features. He was wearing a hood, and while his eyes were completely hidden, Ayato could make out a faint smile.

"What are you doing here?"

"Now, now, Amagiri. Won't you play nice and let me keep you tied down for a while? There's no need for questions." Eishirou, his hands in his pockets, stopped just outside the edge of Ayato's range.

"Let you keep me tied down…? Oh, so that's how it is, is it?" Ayato asked with a slight scowl. His tone made his point clear. "You're siding with the school on this?"

"Well, I *had* wanted to pull back the curtain more dramatically… But I guess it's too late now." Eishirou lifted his hood, flashing Ayato his usual friendly smile as he scratched at the side of his head. "You've heard about Shadowstar, right? Basically, I work for them. Surprised?" he asked with a quiet laugh.

"…Anyone would be surprised to hear that their friend works for an intelligence organization."

"You look pretty calm, though," Eishirou pointed out.

"I guess I've known for a while that you're no ordinary student, Yabuki," Ayato answered as he reached for his waist. "And I did think it was pretty unusual that you weren't interested in taking part in the Festa."

"Hah, is that so…? Looks like I need to up my training." Eishirou lowered his shoulders, crestfallen. "But still, I'm glad to hear you consider me your friend. I feel like I've been deceiving you this whole time." Eishirou's head was drooped, but there was a probing glint in his eyes.

"Hmm… *Conceal* is probably a better way to put it, I'd say. And besides, there are things I've concealed from you as well, so I guess we're both guilty."

At this, Eishirou stared back at him in silent astonishment for a moment. “I always knew you were softhearted, but come on, this is a bit much…”

“That’s not it. I know what I’m doing. I mean, if you’re my friend, you might let me go, right?” Ayato replied with a grave expression, bracing himself for the worst.

The air around them suddenly became tense.

“Hey, hey! You trying to scare me?” Eishirou asked, unfazed. “To tell you the truth, though, speaking for myself, I’ve got nothing against doing just that.”

“Huh?”

“I’ve got my own problems, too, you know? My heart isn’t in this job,” he said, shrugging his shoulders in exasperation.

“…Is Shadowstar really okay with its people having such a half-hearted work ethic?”

It *was* an intelligence organization, after all.

“Ha-ha… Of course not. I’m not trying to brag or anything, but I’m kind of the biggest troublemaker Shadowstar’s ever had. I’ve got a bit of a name for myself there, you know?”

“…No, that isn’t something to boast about.”

Even at a time like this, Eishirou didn’t seem to be feeling any sense of tension or nervousness. “You know, it’s different if I get a choice, but I hate being made to do jobs I don’t want to do. And this time, that’s what it is.”

“So you’ll let me go, then, won’t you?” Ayato asked.

Eishirou, however, gave him a broad grin. “Let’s say you do get away. Do you even have any idea where to look for her?”

“Ah… Not yet.”

He didn’t want to admit it, but that was the truth.

“You won’t find her just fumbling around blindly. You know who it is that’s chasing her, right?”

“Aren’t they…? No, more importantly, do you have any idea where she is, Yabuki? Anything at all?”

“Hmm, I’d be lying if I said I didn’t,” he replied simply.

“In that case—”

Eishirou, however, raised a hand, urging Ayato to be silent. "No, no, no. It'll come back to bite me if I tell you that. Far too dangerous."

"Yabuki, Claudia's life is in danger here! Please!" Ayato begged him.

"Well, I do owe the prez, and it's not like I don't want to repay her... All right, how about this?" he said, clapping his hands together as if coming across some great idea. "Amagiri, let's have a match."

"A match...?"

Ayato couldn't help but wonder what Eishirou was thinking, and yet, judging from the situation, he must have been trying to lead up to this from the beginning.

"If you win, I'll tell you where she is. And if I lose, it'll give me a good excuse to give to the brass... And you know, I've been looking forward to this opportunity for a while now."

"We don't have time for this, Yabuki...!"

"I guess I can't tell you, then."

"Ngh...!"

Eishirou continued to watch Ayato with his usual carefree grin. His eyes, however, were serious. It was clear he wasn't bluffing—and that he wouldn't be willing to negotiate.

"Haah... Fine. What kind of match?"

It looked like he would have no choice.

"Let's see... I don't quite feel like staking my life on it, so how about we do it empty-handed, no weapons? You win if you can take me down."

"And if you win...?"

"I'm just supposed to keep you tied down, so let's just say the longer this thing drags on, the better I can fulfill my job."

Ayato couldn't help but feel as if he had been tricked into reaching this position, but there was no turning back now.

"As for the place... How about that building over there?" Eishirou glanced around before pointing to an abandoned building nearby—the sort of dilapidated construction that you could find just about anywhere in the redevelopment area. It was four stories high, but parts of walls and ceiling around the top floor looked to have already given way to the elements.

"Fine. Sorry about this, but I'm not going to go easy on you."

"Good. Just don't underestimate me," Eishirou replied, before disappearing back into the fog.

"All right, then..."

With that, Ayato released his seal and approached the abandoned building.

*

"Huh...? What just happened?"

In the corridor on the top floor of Queenvale Academy for Young Ladies' Twin Hall, Sylvia tilted her head in confusion as she inspected her mobile.

She had been talking normally until just a few moments ago, but all of a sudden, she seemed to have lost reception. For a second, she wondered whether it had malfunctioned, but the connection had dropped too suddenly for that.

She could try to work out what had gone wrong with it, but she wasn't particularly good at using machines, and to be honest, she didn't know a lot about how they worked, either. Nonetheless, she stood there, playing around with it, trying to get it to reconnect, when—

"...Who were you speaking with just now, Sylvia?"

"Ah! Petra!" She spun around, only to see Queenvale's chairwoman, Petra Kivilehto, walking toward her.

"No, it's nothing... I guess it's not going to work," she murmured to herself, hiding the device behind her back.

She probably wouldn't be able to talk her way out of this one, though, she thought, and so resigned herself to facing her elder. "I was talking to Ayato. Is there anything wrong with that?"

"Ah... I already told you not to interfere with this, Sylvia. You might be the world's most popular songstress, but you understand that even that won't help you if you go up against the wishes of W&W, don't you? Not even I would be able to protect you then."

"I—I know..."

"Then take my advice."

Seeing no other alternative, Sylvia put her mobile back into her pocket.

She wanted to help Ayato as much as possible, but as far as she could see, there wasn't anything she could do for him right now.

"But still, the wishes of the foundation...?"

"What are you trying to say?" Petra's expression, half concealed behind her visor-like pair of glasses, visibly stiffened.

"Nothing. I'm just a little disappointed."

The life of Seidoukan's student council president was now in danger because of the will of an IEF. Not only that, but just when she had thought the other foundations were ready to step in and bring a stop to it, they had all decided to stand aside and watch them kill her in silence. She couldn't help but wish ill upon the whole lot.

"They're as self-serving as you could get, every one of them..." She cursed them all under her breath.

Petra let out a weak sigh. "You're still young, Sylvia. It isn't just the integrated enterprise foundations. As soon as people find a way to better benefit themselves, they all become self-serving. It's only natural. And in this world, that isn't considered wrong."

"I don't know... Not me, at least," Sylvia murmured, as if trying to convince herself.

She couldn't help but think that, in the end, every student at Asterisk was no more than a pawn for the integrated enterprise foundations to profit off of.

Even students like herself, who were afforded more liberties than most others, were simply granted a slightly larger cage from which they couldn't escape.

"...You know, Petra, this has just reminded me that it all boils down to nothing more than a big charade."

"There's no use holding on to that sentimentality of yours, Sylvia. You decided for yourself to become an idol."

"That might be so...but I don't think it's that easy. You understand, don't you, Petra? You were a student here, too."

Petra remained silent for a long moment, before answering in a somewhat muffled tone: "...I've forgotten. It was a long time ago."

Liar, Sylvia thought.

There was no point, however, debating it any further. It would be unfair for her to take her anger out on the older woman and would only end up making her feel worse.

At the very least, she could pray for the safety of the one who was willing to stand up and fight. "Ayato... Hang in there."

*

It was all but impossible to see inside the abandoned building. There was no lighting, of course, and the fog seemed to have seeped within the walls as well.

No sooner had Ayato stepped inside than he noticed something disconcerting.

I can't sense anything...

The Amagiri Shinmei style's perception-expanding technique, the mental state known as *shiki*, seemed to be completely ineffective here. That, too, was probably due to Eishirou's concealment techniques.

"This isn't good..."

But there was no use fretting over it, he told himself.

He glanced across the room, trying to make out his surroundings through the dim fog. In front of him, there looked to be an empty corridor. He could make out a flight of stairs in the back, along with a door hanging from its hinges on the far wall, so damaged that it looked as if it might collapse at any moment.

Relying on the weak light peeking in through the window to guide his steps, he began down the debris-strewn corridor, when something came flying out toward him.

"Ha...!"

He managed to snatch it out of the air before it could hit him. It was a long, slender piece of metal—a *bou-shuriken*.

"...What was that you said about doing this empty-handed, Eishirou?" Ayato called out into the fog, his voice filled with disgust.

"I *am* empty-handed," Eishirou called back. "Unfortunately, it looks like someone's gone and set traps all throughout the building.

I've got no idea who could've done it, but it looks pretty dangerous. You'd better watch out."

"You really are shameless...," Ayato murmured, but there was no use complaining. He would just have to be careful.

He could hardly even make out his own feet, but he proceeded through the building step-by-step, paying full attention to his surroundings.

He had made it almost to the middle of the corridor, when all of a sudden, he sensed a sudden rush coming up from behind him.

"Ngh!"

He rolled forward to evade Eishirou's knife-hand strike, the attack grazing past him.

"Heh, so you dodged it. Looks like you live up to your name, Amagiri. The Phoenix wasn't all for nothing, eh?" Eishirou gave a relaxed laugh.

"You as well. I couldn't sense you at all... What's the trick?"

"Heh, attacking from the shadows is our specialty. If people could see it, that'd leave us in a bit of a bind, don't you think?" Eishirou said, before once again fading away into the dimly lit fog. "This whole place is completely under the control of my techniques. You can't even enter your state of *shiki*, right?"

"I *thought* you'd done something... You keep saying *technique*. Are you a Dante, Yabuki?" Ayato called out, hoping to keep the conversation going so he could detect Eishirou's location.

"I guess you could say that, in a general sense. It's more like Jie Long's *seisenjutsu*, though. But unlike them, only my clan can use these ones."

"Your clan?"

"My family's been involved in this business for a *long* time. They've been teaching me practically since I could walk. My dear father's taken it to heart that those without talent don't deserve to live, so I guess you can say it would have been against his nature to go easy on me. You wouldn't guess how many times I ran away from home..."

The voice was coming from Ayato's right side. Just as he began to turn around to face it, a low spinning kick knocked him off his feet.

The attack had taken him completely by surprise. Even so, he landed on his right hand, twisting his body through the air, and leaping to safety with a backward somersault.

"Heh-heh, you'd better be careful, Amagiri. Making our voices sound like they're coming from somewhere else is child's play for us." This time, the voice came from directly overhead.

"...Thanks for the advice."

Ayato finally understood.

Eishirou Yabuki was formidable.

He might have already known the location of their duel, and laid down traps, but the skill of his attacks and the way he moved were exceptional, easily comparable to those of a Page One.

Fortunately for Ayato, Eishirou wasn't trying to escape, but rather, he was proactively trying to land his own strikes.

If what he said was to be believed, his goal was to delay Ayato for as long as possible. In that case, his best option would be to remain hidden and force Ayato to find him.

Unless that isn't his goal...? No, there's no time to worry about that.

Ayato steadied his breathing, trying to concentrate on his surroundings.

No matter how Eishirou tried to hide his presence, Ayato could still sense him just before he tried to launch an attack. That being the case, the real question was how fast he was able to respond.

He steadied the beating of his heart, letting his prana course through his body.

And then—

"...You're mine!"

"!"

Once again, Eishirou rushed forward from behind with a knife-hand strike—Ayato just barely having enough time to leap out of the way. The attack, however, still hit him in the side, but he did his best to endure it.

He spun around, using the momentum to deliver a strike with the back of his fist into Eishirou's chest.

"Aha!"

Eishirou parried the strike, deflecting it to the side, before immediately lashing out with a powerful sideways kick. Ayato blocked that in turn by crossing his arms together above his head, before pushing Eishirou's leg out of the way with his right hand and delivering an openhanded strike with his left.

Punch met with punch, kick met with kick, the sounds of the contest echoing throughout the abandoned building.

They seemed to be evenly matched in both offense and defense, almost as if they had long been sparring partners.

Ayato continued to watch patiently for an opening, when, finally, as Eishirou unleashed a wide-ranging kick, he spotted one.

"...Now!"

"Wha—?!"

And yet—

He's not there?!

The strike should have been perfectly timed, however, it cut through no more than thin air.

Or more precisely, Eishirou's jacket was still there, but Eishirou himself was nowhere to be seen.

"A substitute...?!"

"Ka-ha, too easy!"

At that moment, a flurry of blows came speeding toward him out of the fog, striking him in his temples, the pit of his stomach, and his thighs in quick succession.

"Guh...!"

He concentrated his prana in an attempt to defend himself, but the attacks had left those vital areas aching. Moreover, Eishirou seemed to have poured his own prana into his attacks, much like Jie Long's martial artists. That wasn't a difficult technique in and of itself, but there was no way it could be carried out so smoothly without a high level of training.

But Ayato couldn't give up. Without so much as pausing, he immediately unleashed a spinning counterattack of his own in the direction that the strikes had been launched.

"Ugh!"

This time, he seemed to have hit something, although judging by the force of the impact, Eishirou appeared to have defended himself against the full force of it.

"Heh… You're quick on the uptake, huh?" Eishirou's voice echoed around him. "Looks like I'd better be a bit more careful."

What could be more careful than this?

He crouched down, bracing himself so he would be able to deal with any possible attack, when he heard an uncanny sound, almost as if something was breaking apart around him.

He glanced at his surroundings, but there didn't seem to be anything out of the ordinary.

No… Wait… That's not it!

"…Above?!" he inadvertently called out, just as a web of cracks began to run the full length of the ceiling—and then it came crashing down.

Ayato raced through the corridor as debris of every size imaginable came pouring down toward him, only bothering to dodge the largest of pieces. Chunks as large as his fist struck his body, but he was in no frame of mind to worry about that.

When at last he reached the stairway, he thought he was finally out of the line of direct fire. But his heightened senses suddenly detected a trap being activated.

A volley of *bou-shuriken* shot toward him from three separate directions. The trap was clearly designed to entrap him in the middle, and it would only really be effective if he was to approach from the direction that he had.

Which meant…

He brought down the ceiling just to lure me here…?!

The debris had come down in such a way as to restrict his movements, forcing him into the snare. He couldn't help but admire the meticulousness and effort that must have been put into it.

There was no way he would be able to dodge the oncoming projectiles, so he had little choice but to concentrate his prana into his arms and stop them from hitting anywhere vital.

"*…Ugh!*"

The damage wasn't serious, but it was enough to bring him to a stop.

And at that moment, he sensed a wave of enmity rushing up from behind.

"It's over, Amagiri." Eishirou's voice, seemingly convinced of victory—cold and calm, and without even the slightest hint of inattention—echoed in his ears.

He may well have been right.

That was, if Ayato hadn't already predicted his next move.

"Wha—?!" Eishirou's face twisted in dismay.

No sooner had he appeared behind him than Ayato had already begun to launch a counterattack.

He struck Eishirou's jaw with the palm of his hand, while at the same time driving his elbow into his chest, before following through with three powerful punches into his stomach.

"Amagiri Shinmei Style Grappling Technique—*Divine Thunder!*"

"*Ugh!*"

And with that, Eishirou, his eyes wide open, came crumbling forward.

"Are you all right, Yabuki?" Ayato called out.

"Ouch… Looks like I lost." Eishirou, his voiced filled with pain, somehow managed to turn onto his back to look up at him.

The sense of animosity that Ayato had previously felt from Eishirou had completely vanished, leaving in its place, rather, a refreshed countenance.

"Tell me one thing, though, how did you know what I was going to do?"

"If I had to put it down to anything, it was just a hunch…"

"*Just* a hunch?"

"Well, with both of your previous attacks, you came from behind, right? So I guessed you'd do the same thing that time, too," Ayato replied.

"Argh, so that was it… I guess I messed up!" His tone suggested that he was joking, but Ayato could tell he felt truly chagrined.

"That pride will get the better of you… Or is it just an excuse?" Ayato didn't know whether to be impressed or dismayed. "Anyway, something's been bothering me for a while now."

"What?"

"Did you really go all out? It didn't seem that way to me."

"What are you talking about? I put everything I had into it," Eishirou said with a giddy laugh.

The reaction rang hollow in Ayato's ears, but now wasn't the time to argue the point.

"So, Yabuki. Where's Claudia?"

"Ah, right. The prez… She's in the harbor block," Eishirou answered, as promised.

"You mean the one surrounding Seidoukan?"

While the harbor block that surrounded Seidoukan Academy belonged to the school, strictly speaking, students weren't normally permitted to enter it. Its main use was for storage, making it more or less a warehouse area.

"Given who's going after her, the worst move would be to let her escape into the city. Even Galaxy would have a hard time hushing it up if anything happened out in public. But then, there are no Festa events today, either, so they'd stand out too much if they tried anything on campus. So that leaves the harbor block. It's the most logical choice."

"I see…" Now that he knew where to look, he couldn't afford to delay any longer. "Eishirou, I—"

"Don't worry about me," Eishirou interrupted. "You should be more concerned about your own safety, if you're planning to go after her, that is." He flashed Ayato a grim smile. "The people after the prez—Galaxy calls them the Night Emit… But they used to be known as the Yabuki clan."

"The Yabuki…?" Ayato repeated, sucking in his breath.

"Yep. And the guy in charge is my very own father."

CHAPTER 5
AFTERNOON

"...*Haah!*" Claudia deflected the Kinoe's dagger with the blade in her right hand, using the one in her left to lash out with a horizontal strike.

Her assailant fell to the ground without a sound, a pool of red blood spreading around it.

The wound wasn't deep enough to put her assailant's life in danger, but nor was it so shallow that they would be able to continue after her right away.

After confirming the situation, Claudia spun around and began to run deeper into the warehouse section. Her uniform was torn in places and stained with blood, but she was fortunate to have been able to avoid suffering any serious injuries.

The sky was hidden behind thick, leaden clouds, with rain beginning to fall. According to the weather forecasts, it was only expected to grow stronger.

Claudia carefully avoided the cameras, set throughout the harbor area at regular intervals, before deciding to hide for a while in a large, dome-shaped warehouse that was filled with row upon row of stacked shipping containers. The huge entrance door was open, as an autonomous vehicle was busy ferrying containers inside—but Claudia, of course, had already known that.

Thanks to the guaranteed employment security offered by the

integrated enterprise foundations, the harbor blocks belonging to the city proper were filled with workers, but in those belonging to the six schools, everything was painstakingly automated.

"Whew... This is rather intense," Claudia said to herself, leaning on a nearby container as she let out a long sigh, trying to catch her breath.

She had been on the move for nearly half a day by then, ever since the attack on her at dawn. She had thought she was ready for it, but the exhaustion was catching up with her.

The Yabuki clan was as good as was to be expected of a combat group under Galaxy's direct control. Claudia had only been able to evade them as successfully as she had thanks to her early preparations and the Pan-Dora's precognition.

But at this rate, she didn't know how long she would be able to hold out.

"...Looks like there's no signal," she murmured as she tried repeatedly to use her mobile, before giving up and returning it to her pocket.

The Yabuki clan possessed a number of skills exclusive to members of their lineage. Some of the worst were their abilities to create barriers that could stop anyone in their tracks and even block out sound and electromagnetic waves. Worse still was the fact that those techniques consumed hardly any mana or prana at all. As such, unlike the abilities of Stregas or Dantes, they were all but impossible to sense.

"I suppose that the situation *is* more or less as I should have expected..." Claudia forced herself to smile, her hands tightening around the hilts of the twin swords.

Just a little while longer.

Just a little while longer, and her wish would be granted.

The only dream she had ever truly wanted.

The selfish wish of a someone who no one fully understood.

It was almost within her reach.

"...I can't afford to die now, not here."

Given that she was, of course, putting everything she had into it, the only thing left for her to do was wait to see which of her innumerable overlapping plans would bear fruit.

After all, her opponent, the Yabuki clan, had hundreds of years of experience in its favor, and then there was its leader, Bujinsai.

It was probably fair to say that this was the most challenging predicament Claudia had ever found herself in.

And yet, she couldn't stop her lips from twisting into a vague smile.

It wasn't her usual, perfect smile, but something else, something purer, and—

"—*!*"

At that moment, she leaped upon a nearby container.

A barrage of *shuriken* tore into it, clearly flying after her in pursuit, but Claudia remained one step ahead.

She raced across the top of the container as fast as her legs could carry her, scanning her surroundings to make out her pursuers, moving soundlessly like shadows.

With the Kinoe being as strong as they were, she would probably have been able to prevail in a one-on-one fight, but two together was a dangerous combination, and with three, escape was the only sensible option left open to her.

"One, two, three...four. I guess this must be one of the Thirty-Six Stratagems," she murmured, leaping out of the warehouse and back into the pouring rain.

She might have been able to do something if she had been willing to use the Pan-Dora's precognition, but she wanted to save that ability not for attack, but for survival.

That being the case, all she could do was keep on running.

*

"—"

"Hmm, this girl's more troublesome than I was expecting," Bujinsai, after listening to a report from one of the Kinoe, whispered to himself.

From his position atop a huge crane overlooking the harbor block, he cast his gaze through the rain and over the gray, hazy scenery that lay before him, the gloom eerily reminiscent of a graveyard.

"Just as I feared... Slipping up at the beginning really has worked against us... That idiot son of mine. No matter how much I hammer it into him...," Bujinsai grumbled to himself as he stroked his chin. There could be no doubt that their target had been tipped off by Eishirou. "To think that he'd rebel against me like this... It's infuriating. If he wasn't so talented, I'd have given up on him years ago."

Shadowstar, Eishirou included, was currently supporting Bujinsai and the rest of the Yabuki clan. The other members might serve their purpose, but Bujinsai had his doubts that his son would do as instructed.

The Yabuki clan specialized in espionage and assassination, not military force. It was fair to say that they had committed an irredeemable blunder the moment they had failed to eliminate the target when they had first engaged her.

That said, even if the target wasn't the school's second-ranked fighter, she was still, after all, a student. He had by no means been underestimating her, but he had never expected her to be able to fend them off for so long.

Things had been going well up until they had cornered her in the harbor block, but now that he thought back on it, there was something off about how everything had played out. The target seemed to be too well-informed.

The harbor block wasn't the kind of place people frequently stumbled into, but they had nonetheless put up barriers to keep out any unwanted visitors. They had also taken control of the security cameras that practically littered the area. One might say that there could be no better field for chasing down one's quarry.

Yet, despite all that, the target had managed to evade their net, as if she knew the precise location of every single security camera.

She showed no hesitation in selecting her escape route, almost as if she were as familiar with it as her own backyard.

She might have been the student council president, but it was incomprehensible that a student, who ought to have had no connection whatsoever to the harbor block, could be so knowledgeable about its layout.

Could it be that she led *us here...?*

On top of that, her combat abilities were more advanced than they had imagined.

More troublesome than her physical skills was the precognition offered to her by the Pan-Dora, which she seemed to be able to use at will. Bringing her down was always going to prove difficult.

And yet, even taking all these factors into account, they still ought to have been able to corner her hours ago. In other words, based on Bujinsai's view of the situation, there had to be another element at play, something that remained yet unclear.

"Where are our scouts? And the ones I sent to circle around south? They're late reporting back."

"We seem to have lost contact with them a short while ago—"

"—!"

Bujinsai suddenly leaped backward, the Kinoe to whom he had been speaking jumping forward to shield him. At that moment, a fast-moving figure suddenly appeared out of nowhere, landing a powerful kick on the Kinoe and sending it hurtling down from the top of the crane before it could even attempt to defend itself.

"..."

The face of the figure who had attacked so viciously, without making so much as a sound or betraying her presence, was hidden behind an unsettling mask.

She landed atop the tip of the crane and silently turned toward Bujinsai.

"Hmph, that mask... You're Jie Long's brat, then?" Bujinsai asked, his eyes narrowing as he slowly stroked his chin. "This might be the harbor block, but this place belongs to Seidoukan. You've got a lot of gall to creep in here, Seiten Taisei."

"...HEH, SO MY FAME PRECEDES ME." The woman—Alema Seiyng—replied not with a voice, but through text displayed on an air-window, as she removed her wolf-shaped disguise and flashed him a broad grin.

"To think that a former number one like yourself has fallen so far, relegated to working behind the scenes as the Ban'yuu Tenra's loyal hound… I really do feel sorry for you."

"You've got a sharp tongue, old man. I guess it's all a lie, that saying that folk mellow with age." Alema, unmoved by Bujinsai's provocative greeting, continued to grin right back at him.

…Hmph. So she didn't rise to the bait.

She had a lot of nerve—as perhaps should have been expected from someone who had been Jie Long's strongest student up until the Ban'yuu Tenra had usurped that position.

"Are you sure you want to do this? Your actions are in clear violation of the Stella Carta. If anyone was to find out, even Jie Long won't come through this unscathed."

According to the Stella Carta, students were expressly forbidden to enter the grounds of the other schools without prior permission—all the more so when such students belonged to one of the schools' intelligence organizations.

That said, from a security point of view, it wasn't actually difficult to do so, as long as one kept away from the central areas of each campus.

Nonetheless, the schools continued to abide by that rule, to avoid the kind of information war that had erupted during Asterisk's early years, which had ended up having a deleterious effect on the operations of the Festa. As such, it had become convention for them to go so far as to tip one another off when one of their own students violated it.

For an agent from one school to enter the grounds of another, that alone was enough to incur heavy repercussions.

"More to the point, there's no benefit here to be had by Jie Long, no matter what you do," Bujinsai added.

"Ha! Listen to yourself!" Alema laughed back at him. "We're not like those spineless clowns you all keep. At Gaishi, we don't have anything to do with benefiting IEFs or schools. We're just the Ban'yuu Tenra's hands, doing as we're instructed. Same goes for you guys, right? We're both pros, huh?"

"...Hmph, you're a boastful one, aren't you?" Bujinsai remarked with a faint smile. "Still, you look more promising than my idiot son."

"I'm actually pretty disappointed, ya know? Your guys were pretty easy. I was hoping for more."

"I see. So it was you who took them out."

Alema Seiyng was, after all, the former number one at Jie Long Seventh Institute.

And unlike the major PMCs and elite brigades belonging to the foundations, both of which enlisted only the finest graduates and fighters, the Yabuki clan's members belonged to a lineage with the power to employ only certain special techniques. Based on individual fighting ability alone, it wasn't surprising that Alema would be able to defeat them.

But even so, they shouldn't have been that weak as to fall victim so quickly to only one person.

"...Fine. At any rate, I don't have time to waste sparring with you," Bujinsai said just as a row of shadows appeared in front of him on the crane.

From the girl's position, a melee on this kind of footing would be unwise. The Yabuki had an overwhelming advantage.

"What's this? There's still this many left? I thought you Yabuki folk were supposed to be just a few elites...? Huh?" Alema tilted her head to one side, her expression one of curious astonishment. "This ain't right. You there—and you...you too—I'm pretty sure I strangled the life out of you just a little while back."

Four Kinoe had surrounded her. They were each dressed identically, and it was impossible to make out their faces. Of course, there were differences in their statures and builds, but for her to be able to recognize them all so quickly was quite a feat.

"My people are unusually sturdy."

No sooner had Bujinsai finished speaking than the four Kinoe burst into action, attacking simultaneously from all sides, seemingly without paying any attention to their own defense—just as they had when they had captured Eishirou the previous day.

And yet, Alema, through some miracle, managed to deflect them all.

She leaped from the tip of the crane at her right, brushing aside the black-coated blade that came toward her with her right hand, while at the same time twisting her body around and using her left hand to snatch the *bou-shuriken* that came hurtling toward her from midair. She then moved to trip over the Kinoe that had come charging at her from in front, before repelling a kick that had come from behind, using her left arm as a weapon in and of itself.

Had her timing been off by even a fraction of a second, she wouldn't have been able to pull it off.

Alema's smile was one of pure joy. For her, the Kinoe weren't enemies.

She struck at the one that had attacked from the front with the palm of her hand, sending it flying through the air, while she placed a fingertip on the neck of the one that had attacked from her right, its body going stiff as it flew into the next crane.

She used her momentum from the kick to launch herself through the air and threw the *bou-shuriken* in her hand back at its caster without so much as a backward glance, scoring an immediate hit. Landing behind the remaining Kinoe, she effortlessly dodged its attacks and launched into one of her own, digging both hands into its abdomen. An intense shock ran through the Kinoe's body, which then dropped silently off the edge of the crane.

"Hmm, not bad."

Bujinsai was legitimately impressed by the complex sequence of attack and defense.

Her skills in the martial arts, polished to a frightening degree, were worthy of the highest praise.

"Compared to Xinglou, you guys might as well be dead weights." Alema sneered, her breathing so regular and calm that it was as if nothing had happened. "I've had enough of these appetizers. Let's move on to the main course." Alema trained her eyes on Bujinsai, pupils glittering with malice.

The man stared back at her calmly, seemingly disinterested, as he scratched his head. "...You're strong. There's no doubt about that. But you are unwise to look down on your elders, girl."

"Oh-ho, what are you gonna do about it?" Alema smirked, lowering her body to attack.

"Be grateful. I'm going to give you a lesson," Bujinsai responded, beckoning with his hand.

*

"Haah... I wonder how Alema's doing...?" Hufeng murmured as he watched the drizzling rain from a corridor in the Hall of the Yellow Dragon.

"Oh-ho, are you worried about her? How unusual." Xinglou, walking in front of him, came to a stop. She turned toward him with an innocent smile.

"It's not her I'm concerned about! It's the institute! Don't you understand, Master? If she slips up, and it can be traced back to us... No, I guess that would still be better than the alternative... If things go wrong, and she gets captured by Seidoukan, it'll turn into a huge problem!"

"Oh my, you're a worrier, aren't you? They're involved in something shady themselves, so even if something was to happen, there's little chance they would dare to go public with it. And besides—" Xinglou paused there for a brief second, glancing up at the somber sky. "I have confidence in her strength and ability. As far as martial arts go, she's no less skilled than Xiaohui."

"That's... I'm aware of that, but still..." Hufeng bit his lip in frustration.

In other words, Xinglou viewed Alema with higher esteem than he did himself.

Alema had her own style of martial arts, one that incorporated techniques from various schools and that continued to evolve with each passing day. It arose not from a hunger for strength, but a hunger for fighting in and of itself.

It was no mere story that she had challenged every single student within Jie Long and defeated them all. While she didn't participate in the Festa, even now, Hexa Pantheon still ranked her within the top ten fighters in all of Asterisk. The fansite's rankings were determined by ability and were greatly influenced by one's public exposure. As such, the fact that Alema had maintained such a high ranking, despite having been relegated to behind-the-scenes work for some time now, was nothing short of astounding.

"Are you saying that we don't need to worry about all this?" Hufeng asked.

"That isn't what I said."

"Huh?"

"It grieves me to say this, but she's rather dim-witted. She'll probably end up challenging the head of the Yabuki to a duel," Xinglou replied, before continuing down the corridor.

Hufeng, feeling left behind, hurried after her. "W-wait, Master! Are you saying that she has no chance of winning against their leader?"

"I didn't say that. There's a chance she might win," Xinglou answered carefully. "However… The Yabuki clan, just like Fuyuka's, is composed of a unique bloodline, inherited uninterrupted generation to generation. The one in whom that blood flows strongest is chosen as their leader. And with stronger blood, he naturally has the most affinity with their techniques. I don't know how strong the current head is, but at the very least, there's little doubt that Alema won't fare very well against those techniques."

"…And you still sent her, despite knowing that?" Hufeng began, before a sudden, intense pressure bore down on him.

"—!"

The pressure, emanating from Xinglou, seemed to swallow him whole, leaving him unable to so much as breathe.

"…Of course. No matter what happens, it will only make her stronger." Xinglou turned toward him, glaring with eyes that screamed death. "Listen well, Hufeng, and don't forget. I, the Ban'yuu Tenra, am here to train you students of Jie Long. She might not be one of my disciples, but she is promising. And I am willing to use any means necessary to accomplish my goal."

"…I understand," Hufeng gasped in apology. "F-forgive me."

With that, the pressure immediately abated.

"At any rate, if she is to fight him, it shouldn't take long," Xinglou muttered to herself as she turned her gaze once more to the dark, rainy sky. "Who knows? It might already be over."

*

The rain continued to grow stronger.

"Dear me, I wonder if this old body can stand up to this autumn rain?" Bujinsai murmured as he wiped a hand across his brow.

Alema grimaced at the acute pain and cold running through her as the raindrops struck her face. Mustering her strength, she managed to pull herself away from the crater-like impression on the wall of the warehouse, spat out a mouthful of bloody vomit, and rose to her feet.

"Oh, so you can still stand? You look much sturdier than us, that's for sure," Bujinsai said, as through truly impressed, stroking his chin.

In his right hand, he was holding a staff-shaped Lux. It was an unusually designed weapon, in which the circular upper part was comprised of glowing light, with a metal disk lodged inside. Alema had never seen such a Lux before, and it was hard to say that it looked particularly practical.

And yet, her opponent was using it to defeat her so one-sidedly. She hadn't been able to get so much as a single attack of her own in.

Damn it, what's with this old geezer...?!

She steadied her breathing, summoning forth her remaining prana. The pain grew dull as she felt the strength flow through every corner of her body.

I'm all right. I can still fight.

At that moment, a wave of delight gushed up inside her.

Right—that was all that mattered. Whether she won or lost, that came second. She just had to fight—and keep on fighting. Because fighting was what she lived for.

"Are you out of your mind? How can you smile in your situation? What a nuisance."

But without responding, Alema instantly closed the distance toward Bujinsai.

She repeatedly thrust with her fingers toward his throat—but to no avail. She moved on to striking with her fists, her palms, her elbows, even the sides of her feet in a midair assault, flowing from one to the next without pause, but none reached their target. Her attacks, all of which had looked at first as if they would find their mark, each fell short.

And to make matters worse, for some reason she couldn't fathom, she found herself unable to evade *his* attacks, attacks she should have been able to dodge without any particular difficulty.

"Let's end this."

And with that, a slash that Alema should have had no problem brushing aside cut into her neck.

She managed to stop it from digging in too deep, but any more, and it would probably have reached an artery.

Nonetheless, taking advantage of that opening, Bujinsai landed a powerful kick into the pit of her stomach and, as Alema fell to her knees, mercilessly kicked her head backward from below.

It was a powerful blow, enough to send her flying until she landed faceup on the ground.

"Even you, Seiten Taisei, cannot fight forever," Bujinsai said indifferently as he stared down at her.

"...JUST LET ME ASK YOU ONE THING," Alema asked, still lying motionless on the ground. "WERE THOSE YOUR STEALTH TECHNIQUES?"

To be perfectly honest, Alema didn't think there was much difference between her and Bujinsai when it came to normal martial arts.

At the very least, she didn't feel the kind of difference in ability that always led her to despair when she fought against Xinglou. Nonetheless, their duel had been completely one-sided. There had to be some other factor involved.

"Maybe." Bujinsai's response was, as she had expected, completely noncommittal. After a moment, however, his lips curled in a slight smile, as if suddenly remembering something. "Well, there's no way a kid like you, trained by Xinglou Fan as she is now, would be able to see through them."

"As she is now...?"

"The story of my great-grandfather fighting that undying monster has been passed down for more than a century. She's the kind who gets stronger with age but was stupid enough to replace her body with *that*." Bujinsai sneered down at her. "She doesn't even have half the strength now that she did then."

Half?!

The shock of those words was overpowering.

But at the same time, an indescribable sense of elation began to well up inside her.

Still lying on the ground, Alema broke out into a sudden burst of laughter—albeit a silent one.

"Hee-hee... Ah-hahaha! Ah-hahahaha!"

Bujinsai knitted his brows, looking down at her suspiciously. "What is it, girl? Have you finally lost your mind?"

"No, you've just reminded me how huge the world is! I can't afford to die now, not like this!" she exclaimed, before leaping up and lashing out with a sudden kick.

He dodged the attack without any difficulty, but that was fine.

"Ngh...!"

Just as Bujinsai stepped backward to distance himself from her, Alema ran up the wall of the warehouse to leap atop a nearby crane.

"...Oh, so you've still got something in you, have you, now?" he murmured, as if truly impressed.

"My bad, but I've already kinda finished what I came here to do, so I'll call it quits for now."

Her instructions, as given by Xinglou, had been to support Seidoukan's student council president to give her an opportunity to escape. It was hard to really call it an achievement, but she had immobilized the majority of the Yabuki clan's assassins. One might say that that was enough.

Her most troublesome opponent might still be left standing, but that couldn't be helped.

"You've finished what you came here to do, huh? You're still wet behind the ears, it seems," Bujinsai said, before slowly lifting his arm.

What...?! Alema wondered.

With that, the figures of what looked like several Yabuki clan members emerged behind him, as if seeping out of the shadows.

More figures had emerged from the shadows around the crane, surrounding her.

Reinforcements...? No, they're—

She should have already defeated the vast majority of them. She might not have had the luxury of finishing them off completely, but the wounds she had dealt them hadn't been so light that they should be able to encircle her now.

Which meant—

"...TCH, SO YOU'VE GOT A HEALER WITH YOU, I TAKE IT?"

Alema's eyes caught sight of a long-haired figure waiting behind Bujinsai. She was wearing the same kind of outfit as everyone else, but like the clan's leader, her head was uncovered. It was readily apparent that, as far as raw strength went, the woman was far below the level of all the other members.

The only reason for bringing someone like that on their kind of mission would be for support, and considering the situation, the only sensible conclusion was that she was a healer.

That said, no healer, not even in the best of hospitals, should have had the power to deal with so many people with so many injuries so quickly. There had to be some kind of explanation, some kind of trick...but she couldn't afford to try to uncover it now.

"...TCH, SO I'VE BEEN HAD. LOOKS LIKE I'VE LOST THIS TIME. BUT REMEMBER THIS, OLD MAN! I'LL BE LOOKING FORWARD TO FIGHTING YOU AGAIN SOMEDAY!" Alema declared, before launching herself from the top of the crane and landing on one of the warehouse buildings below.

"Hmph! I don't have time for that!"

The shadows surrounding her wasted no time leaping after her in pursuit. Alema, however, was in no state to be able to deal with them all again.

Well, it isn't like I don't have my last resort... Alema thought, before raising her hands to her throat. *But I can't afford to use it without Xinglou's permission.*

That said, it would be too easy to simply run away.

And she wouldn't be able to show her face to Xinglou if she didn't at least bring back a souvenir.

Alema wondered what she might be able to take with her as she ran across the rooftop, when her mobile began to sound with a message from an unknown sender. It was a custom-made device, capable of receiving messages only from a select number of individuals, so there should have been no need for anyone to try to hide their identity.

She couldn't help but be suspicious, but she wasted no time in opening the data.

What do we have here...?

The rain buffeting her as she continued to run, she hurried to mentally work out her present location on the map of the harbor block that had accompanied the message.

If what was written there was true, she might be able to bring back a good present after all.

*

"...Father, shall I assign more people to the pursuit? I'm a little uneasy leaving only four of us to catch her."

"No, let her go," Bujinsai replied to his daughter, Eika, as he watched Alema disappear into the rain.

Just as Alema had surmised, Eika was gifted with an extremely rare talent for healing. With the help of certain special medicines, her abilities allowed her to guide even the most severely wounded people back to full health in a matter of minutes. They were only effective, however, on blood relatives.

Bujinsai had brought not only his daughter, but two other healers on their present mission. Each were priceless treasures to the Yabuki clan.

"Our top priority is to carry out the mission. Fighting her took up more time than I expected."

It was already approaching evening. They could try to wait until the target had used up all of the Pan-Dora's precognition stock fighting off the Kinoe in waves, but that would take time, and the longer they waited, the greater the risk.

The harbor block might have been largely automated, but it wasn't completely unmanned, nor would the barriers that they had set up to keep people out hold forever. It was entirely possible that yet another third party might attempt to intervene.

He had ordered Shadowstar to close off the whole area, just in case, but Bujinsai's trust for the student-run organization didn't run particularly deep.

At that moment, one of the Kinoe emerged from the shadows of the wall behind him and whispered in his ear.

"—"

"Good grief..." He couldn't say that he hadn't been expecting this, but the report nonetheless wasn't something he had wanted to hear.

"What's happened?" Eika asked.

"Looks like a stray rat has crept in. Those kids in Shadowstar can't even do that much properly." Bujinsai, after sinking deep into thought for a long moment, let out an extended sigh. "There's no way around it. Keep only as few Kinoe as necessary on the target and have the rest focus on eliminating this rat and fill in for Shadowstar."

"Fill in for Shadowstar?" Eika repeated.

Bujinsai shrugged. "It sounds like that rat has some friends holding them down. It could blow up in our faces in the odd chance that they were to get in. I'm putting you in charge. Just don't put yourself in the line of fire."

"Very well... But what will you do, Father?"

"Hmph. Isn't it obvious?" Bujinsai snorted, before seemingly melting into the rain. "Finish the job."

CHAPTER 6
DUSK

"S-sorry I'm late!" Korona stammered as she all but fell into the student council room.

"...What's all that?" Dirk asked.

Korona blinked in confusion, glancing back at him. "What's all what?"

She clearly had no idea what he was talking about.

"I'm asking you what you're carrying!" Dirk repeated in a tone rougher than his usual terse voice.

Not only were Korona's hands full with shopping bags, she was also wearing a large rucksack on her back.

The bags seemed to be filled with books—a rare sight in the contemporary, digital age. They would undoubtedly be quite heavy, but Korona was, after all, a Genestella.

"O-oh, these? I mean, when I heard that I had the day off, I decided to go into the city to do some shopping. It's been so long since I've been able to go. But then the vice president called me and told me to hurry back, so I came straight here rather than stopping at the dorm. To be honest, it *is* pretty heavy, and I *did* think of going back there, but then—"

"Enough!" Dirk interrupted gruffly. It was impossible to tell whether the drivel that she was spewing out was meant as an excuse or an obtuse boast. "Read my fortune."

"Huh?"

"Hurry up and read my fortune, you dim-witted woman!"

"Y-yes sir, s-sorry, right away!" Korona, taken aback by Dirk's angry roar, hurriedly put down her bags and pulled out a set of tarot cards from her uniform pocket.

Lining the cards up on the floor, she nervously cast her eyes up toward him. "Um… I should just augur whatever I see again today… Right?"

"How many times are you going to make me repeat myself?! Get on with it!"

"*Eep!* S-sorry!" Looking as if she might break down into tears at any moment, Korona hurriedly set about putting everything in order.

Korona Kashimaru, Dirk's private secretary, was a Strega with a very special kind of ability.

However, Korona herself had yet to realize that she was a Strega, nor was she registered in the nationwide database.

This was because her ability could only be activated under very specific conditions, and at all other times, she was indistinguishable from any other Genestella.

She had the power to tell the future—in a way that was always contrary to what would actually take place.

In other words, the fortunes that she predicted never came true.

To most, it would no doubt be seen as a completely useless kind of ability. When it came to information warfare, however, it was invaluable.

"Um, well, today… Ah, right! On the way here, I heard that Seidoukan's student council president had gone missing. I'm a bit worried about her, so why don't I try to find out whether she's okay?"

Three conditions had to be satisfied for Korona to use her ability.

The first was that she had to use it during the evening.

"All right, then, I'll get started…"

The second was that Korona herself had to decide what she would augur.

She closed her eyes and began to rearrange the cards; a bluish-white magic circle rose out of the floor around her.

And the third was that she could use her ability only once per day.

"Okay, here we are!" she exclaimed as she finished turning over five cards and opened her eyes.

"What does it mean?"

"Right, just hold on a minute… Huh?!" Korona, checking the cards, let out a squeal of surprise and leaped backward.

Her actions, as usual, were carried out to excess.

"What does it mean? Come out with it!" Dirk pressed.

The young woman frowned uneasily. "Um, it's… How should I put it…?"

She glanced about at her surroundings, before moving to whisper in Dirk's ear, as if afraid of being overheard.

"…*Tch!* Are you sure?" Dirk clicked his tongue, fixing her with a glare.

"*Eep!* That's what they say!" Korona stepped back, nodding repeatedly.

Dirk, however, was no longer paying attention to her, wrinkling his forehead in consternation. "Damn it… What the hell are they doing?"

*

Seidoukan Academy's harbor block was wrapped around the campus but separated from it by a large canal-like trench, and so it was not usually accessible. Unless one tried to swim across to it, there were normally only three ways in.

The most obvious was to enter via boat. As the harbor block was used to store goods ferried in from the cities on the shores of the lake or brought in from the airport, this was perhaps the most frequently used route.

The next way was to enter aboard one of the many vehicles from the urban areas that were used to move goods around the city.

The last route was an underground passage connected to the center of the academy. Strictly speaking, this was the same route used by the vehicles, but there was an adjoining path that could be entered on foot, too, if need be.

If a student wanted to enter the harbor block, the only practical option available to them was this underground passage.

It was this path, next to the automatic conveyor belts, that Ayato, having regrouped with Julis and the others, was presently hurrying along.

"...Who would have imagined that Yabuki works for Shadowstar?" Julis, running beside him, murmured gravely.

"He had me completely fooled, the way he goes around acting like an idiot all time," Saya agreed, pouting in indignation.

"Now, now, it's thanks to him that we've made it this far."

The underground passage was for use only by the academy's staff and wasn't indicated on any campus maps. If Eishirou hadn't told them about it, they would have had to waste considerably more time just to make it to the harbor block.

"Right. We can deal with him once this is all over and done with. For now, we need to focus on finding Claudia as quickly as possible..."

"Um... Isn't that the way out?" Kirin, running behind Ayato, pointed ahead of them.

Ayato lifted his gaze and found that the path ahead was indeed growing brighter. "All right, let's hurry!"

They all nodded in agreement, increasing their speed, until, finally, they emerged into the open.

"...The rain's gotten pretty bad," Saya noted with a frown as the water began to beat against them.

Sunset was still some time away, but their surroundings had already grown dim. Huge warehouses and tall cranes stood illuminated by yet larger industrial streetlamps. Standing in perfect rows amid the pouring rain, they looked unsettlingly monstrous.

"Now then, we might have made it this far, but with the harbor block being as vast as it is, we should split up, and—" Julis stopped there, just as they all sprang in every possible direction.

The next moment, a huge container, almost as large as a house, came crashing down on the very place where they had been standing. Having dodged it by the skin of his teeth, Ayato glanced up to see its crushed and misshapen bulk lying in front of him.

"...My apologies, but I'm afraid I can't let you go any farther."

No sooner had the voice rang out from somewhere beyond Ayato's perception than several more containers came crashing down one after the other. This time, however, instead of falling toward the four students, they came down in a stack, forming a seemingly impenetrable wall.

"What do you say? Won't you all be good now and run along home?" the speaker asked, appearing atop the newly formed wall, staring down at Ayato and the others.

The hooded figure was dressed almost the same way Eishirou had been.

Shadowstar...? No, wait, that voice...

"I don't know who you are, but we won't go easy on you if you don't get out of our way!" Julis shot the mysterious figure a baleful look in return.

The figure, however, merely shrugged in amusement. "Oh dear... What a horrible thing to say, Glühen Rose. Don't tell me you've forgotten me?"

"What?" Julis glared back suspiciously.

Ayato, however, had already realized who exactly they were facing. "It's been a long time, Silas Norman."

"Wha—?!" Julis exclaimed, her eyes opening wide in shock.

"Ah, I would expect no less from the Murakumo. You, at least, remember me." And with that, the figure lowered its hood, revealing an avaricious, gaunt visage.

There was no mistaking that face.

It belonged to Silas Norman, the Seidoukan student who had colluded with Allekant to secretly attack several of his own school's top students, Julis included.

"...Who would have thought they'd let you into Shadowstar?"

"I wasn't given much of a choice. Seidoukan used me as leverage to force Allekant to come to the table with them, throwing away my freedom forever in the process. One wrong move, and I'd spend the rest of my days languishing in a cell somewhere. But then, instead of handing me over, they came to me with a deal," Silas explained, spreading his thin arms wide. His penchant for theatrics, it seemed, hadn't changed. "They told me that they valued my abilities as a Dante and offered me a place in Shadowstar."

"Oh? Good for you," Julis, still on her guard, replied sarcastically.

"Why you...?! What's good about it?! I'm no more than a pawn to be sacrificed, with a noose already tied around my neck! Seidoukan doesn't give a damn about using me up and then casting me aside! It might beat being locked away somewhere underground, but I'm sick of being treated like this!"

"...You've brought it upon yourself," Saya muttered in disgust.

"...But I suppose it isn't all bad. It's thanks to them that I've got this chance now to take my revenge... Incidentally, that warning a few moments ago was just for show. There's no way I'm going to let you leave." Silas, grinning, snapped his fingers, and several more huge containers floated up into the air in response.

Silas's ability gave him the power to control inorganic objects that he had placed his mark upon.

"So you came for revenge? It's all well and good to resent us—although you *should* be grateful—but do you really think you can take us all on by yourself?" Julis glowered, standing ready to act at even the slightest movement.

"Of course not—I'm not that stupid. You've already beaten me once. Which is why...," Silas trailed off as more shadowy figures appeared one after the other atop the wall of crumbled containers. They were all wearing the same kind of hooded outfits, their faces completely hidden.

There were more than a dozen.

"You're all with Shadowstar...?!" Julis muttered in astonishment.

Silas puffed out his chest confidently. "You're all high up in the rankings, so these types of numbers are kind of necessary, don't you think…? By the way, these guys are all much stronger than I am."

"…They don't look like the sort of people we can afford to let down our guards against," Kirin, her hand resting on the Senbakiri, murmured cautiously, her eyes scanning their surroundings.

Ayato had to agree with her. If the Shadowstar operatives were all at the same level as Eishirou, they would certainly have a big problem on their hands.

"Argh! But we can't just abandon our friend…!" Julis declared, activating her Rect Lux as mana began to swirl around her like a tempest.

"Burst into bloom—*Livingston Daisy!*"

With that, a volley of fiery chakrams spread out, swooping toward Silas and his comrades. Behind them, the remote terminals of her Rect Lux carved red lines through the air.

It was a two-pronged long-range attack, a technique that only someone like Julis, who excelled in processing spatial information, could hope to pull off.

"I'll carve a path right through you all if I have to!"

"Ha-ha! That's what I was hoping for!" Silas's voice was ecstatic, echoing darkly in every direction. He blocked the flying chakrams by lifting a container into their path, just as the other operatives all leaped down from the wall of containers to dodge the remaining attack.

They didn't have time to get embroiled in a melee here—they had to find Claudia as quickly as possible. And yet, their opponents didn't look like they would be receptive toward negotiation.

"I guess I don't have any choice…!" Just as Ayato had put his hand on the Ser Veresta, preparing to unleash his full power, he heard Saya's voice behind him.

"…Go, Ayato," she whispered, before aiming the Helnekraum toward a Shadowstar operative who had begun to dash their way.

"Boom."

The blast, however, went wide of the operative.

"Dear me, were you even aiming?" Silas scorned with a laugh.

But that was fine.

"Huh...?!"

Ayato had already started running—straight toward the gaping hole that Saya's overpowered Lux had burned through the wall of containers.

Ayato had understood from the very beginning that that had been her intention.

"D-damn it!" Silas burst out in panic, throwing container after container in Ayato's direction.

He was too slow. Ayato dodged them all without even having to adjust his speed—before sensing a sudden thirst for blood and bringing himself to a screeching halt.

At that precise moment, an operative jumped out from the shadows of the containers, speeding toward him with dagger drawn.

"No, you don't!" Kirin broke in.

Having blocked the operative's dagger with her Senbakiri, she glanced toward Ayato, flashing him a smile.

"In that case, I'll just have to crush you both!" Silas screamed, throwing a container even larger than the one he had used previously toward the two.

"Burst into bloom—*Amaryllis!*"

It, too, however, was soon engulfed in a fiery explosion.

"Julis!" Ayato called out, turning around.

"Go, Ayato!" she shouted back. "If Laetitia was right, you're they key to all this! You need to go find her!" She flashed him a dauntless smile, while at the same time taking on three separate figures with her sword.

"Sorry, everyone! I won't let you down!" he called back to her, before speeding off again toward the opening in the wall.

But before he could reach it, the containers opened one after the next, unleashing a swarm of dolls that each leaped toward the hole to block his way. "I told you, you're not going through!" Silas laughed. "What do you think? I'm not the same person you fought last time! I can control more than three times as many dolls as when we last met! That's right, I can now use more than three hundred of them simul—"

"…You haven't changed at all, Silas Norman," Ayato muttered before plunging straight into the throng of dolls. He didn't even bother glancing toward his opponent.

"Wha…?!"

"Amagiri Shinmei Style, Middle Technique—*Thousand Beaks of Dismemberment!*"

He swung the Ser Veresta with all his strength, twisting his body to follow through with his momentum to take down every obstacle in his path. The Lux, capable of burning through everything it touched, cut through scores of dolls one after the other, casting them off in every direction as it opened a clear path ahead of him.

No matter how many dolls Silas threw against him, they weren't enough to hold him back.

It didn't take him long to reach the opening that Saya had blasted through the wall. No sooner had he reached it than he passed through without so much as a backward glance.

"H-hold up, Ayato Amagiri! We're not done here…!"

Ignoring the whining echoes behind him, Ayato raced through the rain-soaked harbor block.

*

She couldn't afford to let down her guard, not even for an instant.

If she did, no matter how briefly, the old man in front of her—Bujinsai Yabuki—would cut her down in a single stroke.

"Ugh…!" Claudia used the sword in her left hand to deflect Bujinsai's staff, which he had swung toward her legs in an attempt to knock her over, while at the same time thrusting forward with the one in her right hand to constrain his movements. Her opponent, however, had already jumped backward, sending several *tobi-kunai* throwing blades tearing through the rain toward her.

Claudia, having already used her precognition, knew which way to dodge, but she couldn't stop one from grazing past her cheek.

"Haah… Haah…!"

Her breathing was ragged, her face twisted in pain from the many wounds seemingly burning into every part of her body.

The only reason she hadn't already suffered a fatal injury was because of the Pan-Dora's precognition. Its stock, however, was being whittled away second by second by the opponent before her.

I guess I should have expected this from the head of the Yabuki… I knew he was strong, but not to this extent…

The name Bujinsai Yabuki was one that was handed down by tradition, given only to those who had reached a certain level of skill and ability within the clan. As such, there were times when the position went unoccupied.

Claudia had heard, however, that the current Bujinsai had occupied the position for close to forty years now. That being the case, it wasn't difficult to imagine just how skilled he was.

But I still can't let him beat me so easily…!

After all, she had already come this far.

Her dream, which she had been holding on to for so long, was now finally within reach. She wasn't about to let him snatch it away from her.

She mustered her strength, readying the twin swords of the Pan-Dora.

"Hmm… Not bad, young lady. Who could have imagined that you'd make it this far? Even without your Orga Lux, it's quite a feat," he said, staring at her as he stroked his chin.

He wasn't holding himself in a combat stance, but standing, as always, with a normal posture—one that revealed not a single opening.

"But what's the point of struggling? You must understand that the end is settled, no matter how much time you manage to buy yourself. Or is it that even a person of your talents can't bring yourself to give up on life?"

Claudia couldn't help but chuckle at the man's way of speaking. "I truly am honored to receive such praise from a person of your caliber, Bujinsai… But unfortunately, I think that you've misunderstood."

"Oh?"

"You wouldn't understand just how much my heart is racing right now. No, there isn't *anyone* who would understand. Ah, how long I've been waiting for this, how very long…! Not even I could have thought it would be like this…!" Claudia smiled at Bujinsai with all her heart.

"…Good grief." Bujinsai scratched his head. "First that girl from Jie Long, now you. You're all out of your minds in this town."

"Oh dear, are you talking about your son as well?"

"*Ugh*, you know where to hit hard…" The man smiled back in response, his left hand moving suddenly.

Another one…!

Claudia spun around to dodge the *tobi-kunai*, lifting her blade to meet her opponent, who had already closed the distance between them.

Bujinsai parried it effortlessly with his staff, jumping within feet of Claudia and then lashing out with the palm of his hand.

"You're only focusing on defense, young lady!"

"Indeed. My attacks wouldn't work against you anyway…," Claudia answered, leaping backward through the air.

Bujinsai's martial art skills far exceeded her own, putting her at an overwhelming disadvantage.

"Now, now, young lady. Your swordsmanship is clean and sharp. There's no need to be so modest. How will you know if you don't try?"

"I know."

Bujinsai's staff crashed again and again with Claudia's Pan-Dora, sending sparks of mana scattering in the rain.

"Someone like me wouldn't be able to break past the Yabuki clan's secret Void Tide technique, would I?"

"—!" With his staff locked to her swords, Bujinsai's narrowed his eyes in suspicion. "…Where did you hear that?"

"And I've heard that the barriers you use are another application of this Void Tide," Claudia continued without addressing his question. "You use your mana to manipulate people's subconscious actions through combinations of colors and patterns that they have an instinctive reaction toward. It isn't quite mind control, but it comes close."

"..."

All in all, it meant that even if Claudia was going to try to attack him, on a subconscious level, her body wouldn't allow her strikes to reach their target.

The same thing went for defense. If she didn't correct herself after using the Pan-Dora's precognition, she would risk being lured right into the line of fire.

"I can't judge your timing very well, seeing as it starts working immediately and consumes hardly any mana... But that makes sense. As a technique, it dates back to a time when mana was extremely scarce in the world. It's so weak I can barely sense it at all."

The effect was just as imperceptible, too.

Genestellas' heightened levels of mana gave them above-average resistance to mind control techniques, so there was no way that such a small amount would be able to influence them.

This technique, however, played on people's most primal instincts, meaning that that natural resistance had no effect whatsoever.

"But I suppose if all you're going to do is strangle your targets in the dark, you don't exactly need to be able to breathe fire or conjure up demons. I see the logic behind it."

"...Whew..." When she had finished speaking, Bujinsai let out a long, deep sigh.

Claudia felt a chill run down her spine.

That's...! I was trying to buy time, but it looks like I've said too much...

It seemed that she had opened a can of worms.

She tried to move away from her opponent, but for some reason, her body had turned stiff, refusing to move.

Almost immediately, Bujinsai's staff slammed deep into her stomach, leaving her voiceless and throwing her to the ground.

As she rolled across the rain-soaked floor like a ball, Bujinsai cast a flurry of *tobi-kunai* in her direction.

"Ugh...!"

Claudia twisted her body, trying to shake free of the small blades that had pierced her hands and feet, but her movements were cut short when Bujinsai threw yet another volley into her shoulders and thighs.

"Aaaaagh!" she screamed in agony.

The attack might have looked effortless, but his aim was unerring. Claudia could do nothing but writhe on the ground in pain.

"I think I understand why my masters ordered me to take care of you. Your knowledge runs too deep, as if you're peering into our brains." Bujinsai spoke quietly, but his voice was filled with a clear sense of unease.

"Heh, heh-heh... You give me too much credit... I'm no god... *Ugh!*" She forced herself to keep talking, to buy just a little more time.

Bujinsai's expression, however, remained unchanging.

No... At this rate...

She could feel a sense of panic building up inside her.

Not yet.

She needed just a little more time.

"It's over. Your precognition means nothing if you can't move. Now, time to die."

A wave of *tobi-kunai* came hurtling toward her forehead, her throat, and her heart.

It was just like he said. If there was no future in which she could dodge his attacks, her precognition was meaningless.

And yet—

"Ah...! I've been waiting for you..."

Claudia's jubilant smile was covered in mud and blood.

A moment later, she was engulfed in a black whirlwind as the silhouette of a figure wielding a giant sword came soaring to her aid.

CHAPTER 7
EVENING

"Claudia, are you okay?" Ayato called out as he shielded her from her opponent.

He wanted to tend to her wounds as soon as possible, but first, he would have to deal with the danger standing across from them.

"I can't say that it doesn't hurt... But at least my life isn't in immediate danger anymore."

"Right. That's a relief."

In that case, the worst seemed to be over. But when he thought about what would have happened had he arrived even a moment later, he couldn't stop a violent wave of anger from welling up inside him.

"Boy... You must be the Murakumo?" the old man asked softly.

Ayato nodded, raising the Ser Veresta toward him. "And you must be Bujinsai Yabuki?"

"Oh, so you've heard of me?"

"From your son."

Bujinsai scratched at his chin in apparent embarrassment. "Yes, I see. You share a room with that idiot son of mine, don't you? Does he give you any trouble?"

"Please, step aside." Even knowing that the old man would never agree to it, he had to ask.

After all, Bujinsai was his friend's father. He could barely hold down his rage at the thought of what he had been about to do to Claudia, and he would, of course, never be able to forgive him for it, but it would be best for everyone if they could resolve the situation peacefully.

"Ha! You're direct, I'll give you that. Not a bad quality… But I'm afraid I can't oblige." Bujinsai's lips curled into a broad smile as he began to spin his staff in a circle.

Ayato's sense of warning continued to grow more urgent.

"…Then, can you at least give me a minute?"

"Hmm?" The man frowned.

Ayato's sense of warning abated slightly. Taking this to mean that the request had been agreed to, he bent down to face Claudia—without, of course, letting down his guard.

"Ayato…" Claudia, her eyes damp with tears, stretched a hand out to his face.

Placing it softly in his own, Ayato used his free hand to take something out of his pocket. "Claudia, a friend of yours wanted me to give you this."

"Huh…?" Confusion spread across Claudia's almost-feverish face. "What…?"

"It's from Laetitia," he added, placing the silver amulet into her hand. She was so exhausted that she almost dropped it, so Ayato instead put it into her breast pocket. "I think it's supposed to be a good luck charm."

"N-no, I know that… But why…?" She seemed genuinely confused, but before Ayato could ask her why, he sensed a sudden foreboding emanating from just a short distance away.

Bujinsai, it seemed, wasn't willing to wait any longer.

"Sorry, Claudia. It'll be over soon."

"Um…" Claudia reached out to him as if to hold him back, but she quickly relented, flashing him her usual smile. "No, it's nothing. Good luck, Ayato."

Ayato returned the smile, before turning back to Bujinsai.

"My apologies. I don't mean to interrupt your final tryst, but I've got a lot on my plate. I can't afford to waste any more time."

"...That's okay. Because this won't be the last time," Ayato replied casually.

Bujinsai immediately launched into his attack, casting a flurry of *tobi-kunai* in Ayato's direction, along with a volley of *shuriken* arcing down from above. Ayato deflected the blades with the Ser Veresta, about to rush toward his opponent, but during the short instant he'd taken his eyes off him, he had disappeared.

"—!"

If he hadn't fought Eishirou, if he hadn't already been familiar with this strategy of circling around one's opponent's back, that would have been the end of it.

His forward dive to dodge the oncoming strike was all but reflexive, and while he plunged headfirst into a pool of water, that was by far the better of the two options. Had he not done so, his head might have been sliced clean from his body.

"Oh?" Bujinsai, his staff having carved through nothing but air, glanced toward Ayato suspiciously. "Don't tell me you saw that coming...?"

He seemed to have realized how he had done it.

"So be it. In that case, I'll take your head from the front."

Bujinsai's body swayed back and forth, melting into the rain, until all of a sudden, he was standing directly in front of him.

He's fast!

Ayato quickly raised the Ser Veresta to counterattack—when he remembered what Eishirou had told him earlier:

"Are you listening, Ayato? If you're gonna fight my father, let me give you a word of advice. It's practically impossible to land a blow on him. The same thing goes when trying to dodge his attacks. So—"

Ayato readied the Ser Veresta in a defensive stance, concentrating his prana.

"Ugh...!"

"What?!"

The attack, aimed squarely for Ayato's neck, reached its target, but fortunately, Ayato's head was still in place. He had focused his prana on several places throughout his body to increase his defense—the areas not protected by the Ser Veresta, such as his neck, hands, and feet. The older man's strikes were so precise that they ended up being easily read.

Bujinsai recoiled slightly, giving Ayato an opening to slash back with the Ser Veresta and put some distance between them.

He lifted his free hand to his neck. It seemed to be bleeding, but the wound wasn't deep.

"I see. Knowing that you couldn't dodge it, you decided to withstand the blow. I suppose that's only possible thanks to that incredible amount of prana you seem to have."

It was as Bujinsai said—Ayato's defense had consumed such a large amount of prana that if a regular Genestella had attempted it, they would have quickly run dry.

"You must realize that you're only sprinkling water on parched soil. You seem to have some idea about my techniques, but if you pour everything into defense, how will you strike back? Sooner or later, you'll have exhausted everything you have."

"..."

Bujinsai's words were spot-on.

Even if he was able to hold out for a short while, without changing his strategy, there would be no way to defeat the older man.

However—

"Just in case, I prepared two strategies before coming here. Do you want to see them?"

"Oh?"

"Then again, they both involve outright attacks, so maybe strategy isn't the right word."

Ayato tightened his grip on the Ser Veresta, before lashing out with his first one.

Bujinsai jumped backward diagonally, jumping against the side of a nearby crane and onto the platform above.

Ayato chased after him the same way, swinging the Ser Veresta to the side. Bujinsai spun through the air, before landing on the roof of a warehouse—and swung his staff toward Ayato's head just as he landed beside him.

Again, Ayato concentrated his prana to endure the blow, before lashing out with an attack of his own. He sliced upward from below, then downward from above, as his opponent tried to dodge.

The older man's staff-shaped Lux might have been of unusual construction, but it was unable to block against the Ser Veresta. He could do nothing but throw himself in the opposite direction, just as Ayato followed through with another lunge.

This first strategy that Ayato had prepared was to drastically increase the number of his attacks.

It stood to reason that even Bujinsai couldn't keep using his techniques indefinitely. In that case, no matter how many times he managed to dodge them, Ayato simply had to keep pressing the assault, up until his opponent exhausted himself.

"Heh...heh... You're certainly pushing it, calling this a strategy," Bujinsai goaded, continuing to launch his own attacks while dodging Ayato's blade.

Even so, Ayato concentrated his prana and withstood them all, frantically swinging the Ser Veresta at his opponent. His body was taking on one injury after another, and blood was beginning to soak into his clothes, but he couldn't afford to falter.

"Amagiri Shinmei Style, Middle Technique—*Ten-Thorned Thistle!*"

But Bujinsai effortlessly dodged the surprise swing.

"Ha-ha, I know that move!"

"Wha—?!"

During the brief window in which the technique had left him open, the older man lunged out at him with the palm of his hand, throwing him from the top of the roof.

He landed flat on the ground, and while he wasted no time pulling himself to his feet, Bujinsai was already there to meet him.

He's much more powerful than I was expecting...

To begin with, their techniques were at a completely different caliber. If it was to come down to brute physical strength, Ayato would have probably had the lead, but taking into account their respective tactics and the timing of their attacks, the advantage undoubtedly lay with Bujinsai.

On top of that...

"Oh? So you noticed? That's right—I'm familiar with your Amagiri Shinmei style."

"...I see..."

Whether he had mastered the fighting style or not, there would have been no way that he would have been able to take advantage of the opening left by the Ten-Thorned Thistle if that was his first time seeing it.

"My clan has been around for a long time, boy. We've kept records of every opponent that we've faced over the centuries, all passed down and recorded for posterity. And in that time, we've faced several users of your style."

The Amagiri Shinmei style was an old school of swordsmanship, so it wasn't altogether unusual that that should be the case. And it explained how Bujinsai had seen through not only the technique itself, but also the trajectory of his attack.

But in that case, it would probably be difficult to defeat him simply by increasing the number and rate of his attacks.

"Now then, why don't you show me this second strategy of yours?" Bujinsai asked, as if reading his thoughts.

"I don't need you to tell me that...!"

"Oh...?"

"Haaaaaaaaah!"

With an almighty cry and his hands gripping the Ser Veresta as tightly as he could, Ayato poured his prana into the blade.

He was using Meteor Arts.

According to Eishirou, the Yabuki's techniques involved affecting their opponents' subconsciousness to disrupt their actions.

In that case, he would use an attack so large that it wouldn't matter even if his aim was disrupted.

"Yaaaaaaaaaa!"

Ayato poured his prana into the sword, instantly triggering mana excitation overload in its urm-manadite core, causing the blade to extend to more than five yards in length, before swinging it down in front of him.

"Hmph...!"

The blade, however, made contact only with an afterimage of his opponent. Bujinsai, it seemed, had effortlessly evaded the strike. Ayato had succeeded in cutting through only the streetlight behind him, which came crashing down into the lake.

The rain, still pouring around them, evaporated as soon as it hit the long blade of the Orga Lux, causing a haze of white steam to rise up around them.

"I see you've turned to a brute-force approach. Do you really think that gigantic thing will be able to reach me?" Bujinsai scoffed, casting a flurry of at least a dozen more *tobi-kunai* toward him.

"Ugh!"

In its current state, the Ser Veresta was too large to knock them all down. His only option was to leap to safety.

But as if having already anticipated that, Bujinsai suddenly appeared right in front of him.

"I won't let you get away this time. Even if you do try to withstand it, I'll just have to whittle your prana down bit by bit..." The old man's eyes glowed darkly as he approached ever closer.

This was the chance that Ayato had been waiting for.

Letting go of the Ser Veresta and concentrating his prana into his stomach to endure the powerful slash, he clasped his hands around his opponent as strongly as he could.

This is the only way to bring down a faster, more skilled opponent...!

"What?!"

It was the same strategy he had used in a duel against Kirin.

The Amagiri Shinmei style was originally developed to be used by those dressed in full battle armor, and so the purpose of its grappling techniques wasn't to strike one's opponents or knock them aside, but rather to pin them down. After all, once an armored opponent was pushed into the ground, further resistance was all but impossible.

As such, he had resorted to one of his school's oldest and most inelegant moves:

"Amagiri Shinmei Style Grappling Technique—*Twisted Vine!*"

He grabbed Bujinsai's arm, pushing himself toward his opponent as he kicked his legs out from under him.

He was, in short, throwing his whole body on top of him, so it wouldn't matter too much if Bujinsai managed to interfere with his movements.

"Ngh...!"

If Bujinsai was as knowledgeable about the Amagiri Shinmei style as he appeared, he would probably know how to free himself from his situation, so Ayato immediately moved into his next attack, concentrating his prana into his fist and slamming it down into the soldier's chest.

"Amagiri Shinmei Style Grappling Technique—*Divine Hammer!*"

"Koff...!"

Ayato had put so much strength into the strike that the air around him trembled, the shock coursing straight through Bujinsai's body and shattering the ground into a small crater beneath him.

It was a more advanced version of the technique that he had used against Eishirou, made more powerful by his having poured his prana into the attack.

This should do it...

"—!"

But as soon as Ayato, thinking he had snatched victory, relaxed his guard, Bujinsai's eyes suddenly snapped open.

Ayato's body immediately turned stiff, leaving him unable to so much as lift a finger.

A binding technique...?!

Left completely defenseless, Bujinsai drove the palm of his hand into Ayato's stomach.

"Ngh!"

The attack sent him flying through the air, crashing into the ground before he could have any chance to prepare for the impact.

"Serves you right, you damn kid...!" Bujinsai spat out a ball of blood before wiping at his mouth with his fist.

"Now you've gone and done it. I wasn't going easy on you or letting down my guard, but I suppose some part of me wanted to see what you could pull off. I guess I'll have to be more careful." The man's words, finally shedding their false dispassion, rang with indignation.

"Argh..." Ayato forced himself to move, albeit only slightly, but most of his body remained frozen in place. The best he could do was force himself to his feet, though unsteadily.

"It's over for you. The immobilization effect hasn't worn off yet. I'm impressed that you can do this much, but now...," Bujinsai trailed off, balancing his staff against the ground, and effortlessly cast eight separate *tobi-kunai* toward him.

"—!"

Ayato was in no condition to dodge them. Barely managing to raise his hands to protect his face, he poured his prana into his body in an attempt to withstand the blows.

If he couldn't free himself from this binding technique, he was finished.

Continuing to let his prana flow through his body, he glanced between his clenched fingers covering his eyes and caught his breath at the sight of his opponent.

"...I wonder how much you can endure?" Bujinsai murmured, another round of *tobi-kunai* already clenched between his fingers.

He can't mean to do it like this...?!

The man intended to engulf him in a storm of steel.

Each and every one of Bujinsai's endless shower of blades found their targets, tearing into Ayato's flesh, rasping against his bones.

Ayato gritted his teach, trying to weather the pain, but he could feel his prana decreasing at a frightening pace.

"Haah... Haah...!"

But there was nothing he could do. He couldn't even get his body to move as he wanted it.

When finally it came to an end, dozens, perhaps even hundreds of the small throwing blades had struck Ayato's body.

The blades seemed to be composed of some mysterious substance, as they quickly began to soften away in the rain, melting into a puddle of a strange black liquid building up at his feet.

Ayato fell to his knees, letting the strange liquid splash all over him.

His prana had reached its limit. His whole body was covered in wounds.

"...I guess it's time." Bujinsai, staring down at him, raised his staff to deliver the final blow.

Bujinsai approached slowly, without revealing even the slightest opening.

This... This is bad...

Ayato's vision was growing blurred, and though he strove to muster what remained of his strength, he couldn't bring his body to move.

And then—

"Ayato! Get ahold of yourself! You've got more in you than this!"

—Claudia's voice, strong and clear, came rushing toward him.

Her words were filled with confidence. She wasn't merely trying to console or encourage him.

And with that, before he knew it, he had brought himself to his feet amid the darkness.

Or more precisely, he was overlooking himself from above, watching another version of him lift himself up.

This is...

Though at a loss, he immediately understood. He had experienced this before.

He was looking at an image—an image of the chains that bound him.

Like last time, there were three locks attached to the chains. The first lay shattered, the second unlocked. And the third...remained clasped shut.

He slowly unfolded his clenched hand, revealing a glimmering key.

He understood it immediately. The key was still incomplete. It needed more.

Even so, he didn't hesitate to insert it into the third lock. Even if it was incomplete, even if it wasn't enough, even if, like when he first broke the first lock, it only lasted for a short length of time, if he could just break free now...

*

"Now then, let's finish this." Bujinsai raised his staff toward the stormy sky as he prepared to bring it down upon Ayato's exposed neck.

It had taken longer than he had intended, but now he would finally be able to clear away this final obstacle. All that would be left would be to take care of the target, and his work here would be complete.

Or at least, that was how it should have happened.

"—?!"

And yet, the strike, which should have sheared its target's head clean from his shoulders, cut through nothing but air. Ayato, who had been kneeling weakly on the ground, had completely disappeared.

Taken aback, Bujinsai spun around—only to see the boy standing calmly a few yards away.

"When did you…?! No, more importantly…" Bujinsai inadvertently took a step backward, staring at Ayato, who continued to stand motionless in the rain. His face was unreadable, tilted toward the ground, while a powerful force emanated from his body.

His prana had been on the verge of depletion, his body covered in injuries and bleeding profusely, and now he was unarmed as well.

And yet—

I've got a bad feeling about this…

A cold sweat began to run down Bujinsai's back.

He wanted neither to admit it nor to believe it, but his instincts told him he was in danger.

I'm not going to let some kid get the better of me!

Trying to shake off his uneasiness, he cast four *tobi-kunai* toward Ayato to distract him while shortening the distance between them.

The binding technique was another application of the Yabuki clan's secret Void Tide ability, intended to put the subject into a state of extreme tension so they found themselves unable to control their body. Its biggest weakness was that the user had to be looking into the subject's eyes at close range. Bujinsai couldn't work out why it had stopped working, but if he could just activate it once more, he would be able to finish everything once and for all.

"…"

Ayato, in total silence, moved his body slightly to dodge each of the airborne blades one by one.

Bujinsai, of course, had taken such a possibility into account.

The *tobi-kunai* had been no more than a distraction—and one that had given him the opening he needed to get close enough to—

"Gah…?!"

Before he could properly react, however, Ayato's clenched fist slammed into his chin.

I-impossible…! How can he be this fast…?!

He hadn't even had a chance to use the Void Tide technique.

There was no obvious reason for his opponent's change. But despite that, his level of skill had undergone an unfathomable transformation.

What the hell just happened…?!

In his confusion, Bujinsai quickly leaped back to safety.

Only then did he realize what he had done—

He had lost sight of the boy.

And at that very instant, his long-cultivated intuition warned him of a fast-approaching source of danger coming from directly behind him.

That's… That's our technique…!

"Rending the five vital organs and crushing the four limbs—"

Bujinsai spun around, but the voice continued to echo in his ears.

"Amagiri Shinmei Style Grappling Technique—*Nine-Fanged Hammer!*"

At that instant, a tempest of nine consecutive strikes slammed into him, breaking both his arms, crushing his legs, and gouging into his liver, heart, spleen, lungs, and kidneys—the final blow delivered with unimaginable force.

"Gargh?!"

His body went flying into the base of a large crane, the shock strong enough to practically impale him on the machinery.

"*Ugh…* I-impossible! How could this…?"

His broken voice filled with resentment, he could do nothing but watch as Ayato slowly stepped toward him.

*

It was a strange feeling.

He didn't feel as if there was any new power welling up inside him, but rather like he had returned to how his body was supposed to be.

He had merely followed his instincts, and just like that, he had overpowered his opponent.

"...But it's not over yet," he murmured.

Even having been subject to the Nine-Fanged Hammer, Bujinsai didn't appear to have lost his will to fight. He probably wouldn't be able to stop him unless he knocked him unconscious, Ayato thought.

He stepped forward, preparing to deal the final blow—when he suddenly fell to his knees, letting out a terrible scream as an overwhelming pain began to take hold.

"Aaaaaaaaaaaaaagh!"

His time was up.

Magic rings appeared around him, spewing out fresh chains that wrapped about his body.

"N-no! Not yet...!" Ayato let out a mute curse. But his sister's ability was too powerful. There was no way he could resist it.

Bujinsai began to smile, an expression of relief and dead assurance.

He cast a fresh *tobi-kunai* toward him.

In his current state, Ayato could do nothing to dodge it, nothing but watch as the black blade approached, as if in slow-motion. He had fought to the bitter end, but his efforts, it seemed, had come to nothing.

But just before it could reach him—

"Ayato!" Claudia leaped in front of him.

"Claudia!" he cried back, but he was too late.

Fresh blood flowered amid the cold, dark rain.

CHAPTER 8
NIGHT

"Claudia!" Ayato ignored the intense pain running through his body as he swooped down to take her in his arms.

One of Bujinsai's black throwing blades was lodged deep into her chest, blood seeping profusely from the wound to soak her tattered uniform.

"...Are you okay, Ayato...?" Claudia asked weakly, stretching out a hand to brush his cheek as she flashed him a gentle smile.

"I'm okay...! But you, Claudia, you're...," Ayato began, before finding himself at a loss for words. She was in a perilous condition.

"Ah... Sorry, Ayato... Please don't make such a face... You haven't done anything wrong... But I guess... I guess it's no good—me saying that now... I'm sorry, Ayato, truly..." Despite her situation, despite what she was saying, her face wore a look of contentment that Ayato had never seen before. "I'm... It was selfish of me... But finally... I've been able to reach this point in time..."

"Claudia! Hang in there!" Ayato pressed against the wound to try to stem the bleeding, but it didn't help.

"Right... You probably don't know...just how long I've been waiting for this... For this moment...that I saw in my dreams..." She was growing weaker by the moment, her voice hoarse.

Her eyes had already lost their focus.

Tears had begun to trickle from the corners of her eyes, all but indistinguishable from the pouring rain.

"Ah... I'm so happy, Ayato... To me, this... This wonderful moment... No matter how much time passes... This feeling... Forever..." But with that, the hand that was brushing against his cheek lost its strength, falling silently to the ground.

"Claudia!" Ayato cried out again.

But it looked like she had only lost consciousness.

The wound was serious, but if he could get her to the hospital right away, there might still be time. Director Jan Korbel's reputation wasn't unearned.

However—

"Heh-heh... I guess luck is finally turning my way..." Bujinsai chuckled, his shoulders trembling as he staggered forward.

"*Tch...!*" Ayato glared back at him.

"Our target was always that young lady." His eyes glimmering dangerously, the old man bent down to retrieve his staff, all without shifting his gaze away from the two students. "But now that it's come to this, I won't be satisfied until I take your head, too..."

Bujinsai, it seemed, was in no mood to let him go.

He seemed to have suffered grave injuries of his own, but Ayato had reached his limit.

Ayato had no idea how long he would be able to resist him, but he couldn't just sit back and do nothing.

I've got to get out of here, no matter what it takes, and get Claudia to the hospital...

"Hmm...?"

Before Bujinsai could reach him, however, a black-clothed figure suddenly appeared behind him, whispering something in his ear.

"—"

"What...?" The old man's face twisted in displeasure, and he clicked his tongue in annoyance. "*Tch*, fine! We'll pull back!" Seemingly no sooner had he finished speaking than he, along with the black-clothed figure, disappeared into the rain-drenched night.

"...I don't get it... I guess we made it...?"

At that moment, an air-window suddenly snapped open in front of him.

"WELL, LOOKS LIKE BEATING THE CRAP OUT OF THEIR HEALERS TAUGHT THEM A THING OR TWO. AND THOSE LITTLE LADIES HAVE HAD A BIT OF FUN AS WELL, BY THE LOOKS OF IT. OUR FRIENDS PROBABLY CAN'T KEEP THIS PLACE SEALED OFF FOR MUCH LONGER, HEH."

"Wha—?!" Ayato startled as the words flowed silently past. Glancing around, his gaze found its way to a masked woman emerging from behind a nearby warehouse.

He readied himself as best he could for more trouble, but the woman hurriedly raised her hands as if to say that she had no intention of fighting him.

"LOOK, CLEARLY THERE'S NO USE IN ME TELLING YOU TO RELAX, BUT CAN YOU AT LEAST HEAR ME OUT? YOU CAN TRUST ME, YOU KNOW?" The words flowed across the air-window, overwriting those that had been there a moment ago.

"Who are you...?"

On closer inspection, the woman looked to have suffered several injuries of her own—and rather serious ones at that. Just managing to stand up straight must have been quite an ordeal for her.

"I CAN'T TELL YOU THAT, AND YOU DON'T HAVE TIME FOR IT ANYWAY. THE BOAT THAT I USED TO GET HERE IS NEARBY, AND THERE'S A CAR WAITING ON THE OTHER SIDE OF THE CANAL. LET ME GET YOU BOTH TO THE HOSPITAL."

There was no mistaking that, in his present condition, Ayato would have a hard time getting Claudia there on his own, and it was impossible to tell just how long it might take.

"...All right. Thank you," he replied, making up his mind.

The woman nodded. "THEN LET'S GET GOING. SHE DOESN'T LOOK TOO GOOD."

Ayato could see that for himself.

Holding Claudia in his arms, he followed after the woman as she led the way.

"AH, RIGHT. I SAW YOU FIGHTING HIM JUST BEFORE. I GOT A REAL

KICK OUT OF IT, WATCHING YOU BEAT THAT OLD MAN AROUND. YOU'RE PRETTY GOOD, YOU KNOW?"

"Ah..."

"...I THINK I'M GONNA HAVE TO HAVE A GO AT YOU ONE OF THESE DAYS MYSELF." Fortunately, these words appeared in the air-window only for the briefest of moments, vanishing before Ayato could have a chance to read them.

*

"'Fall back'...?!" Silas repeated in dismay.

At the sound of his voice, the melee in which ally was all but indistinguishable from enemy came to a sudden halt.

Julis, breathing heavily, glanced toward Saya and Kirin to see whether they knew what was going on, but the two were just as confused as she was.

"Wh-what are you talking about...?! That's the first I've heard of it!"

Their opponents, however, seemed to be just as bewildered.

Julis and the others were surrounded by Shadowstar's hooded operatives, along with several black-clad figures that had entered the fray—no doubt members of the Yabuki clan.

When they had been facing Shadowstar alone, Julis and the others had been able to take the upper hand—probably because the student-run intelligence organization's first priority was simply to keep them tied down—but as soon as the Yabuki clan had gotten involved, the situation had undergone a sudden reversal, and they had found themselves on the defensive.

In spite of that, thanks to their training for the Gryps, they had been able to hold out. Even in the middle of the throng of combatants, their coordination had been enough to keep them from getting caught in too awkward a position, at times trusting their companions to cover them as they fought their way through the mass of fighters.

That said, it was undeniable that they had been seriously outnumbered from the very beginning.

Moreover, their opponents were each highly capable individuals in their own right.

At the current rate, it was only a matter of time until they slipped up and made a mistake, or weariness got the better of them—until, of course, their opponents had descended into confusion at the sound of Silas's flustered voice.

"You're telling us to pull back, now that we've finally gotten the upper hand?! That's, that's…!"

"—"

The figure standing beside him in silence was undoubtedly a member of the Yabuki clan.

Compared to Silas, he remained perfectly calm, giving a signal to the other Yabuki members, who promptly melted away into the shadows.

"Argh! Fine! We'll fall back as well…!" Silas, his face red, stomped his feet in anger.

The containers that had been floating in the air throughout the fight came crashing down one after another. This time, however, Silas wasn't trying to throw them at the three girls—he had simply released them from his hold.

Julis covered her face with her arms as water filled with concrete shards flew around them.

It must have only taken a few seconds, but by the time she opened her eyes, the Shadowstar operatives had disappeared as well.

Only Julis, Saya, and Kirin remained. They glanced at one another briefly before sinking to the ground in exhaustion.

"Ah… Does this mean we did it…?" Kirin murmured.

"…That was tiring." Saya sighed, deactivating her Lux and lying faceup on the ground.

The three seemed to be in the middle of a huge puddle of water, but seeing as they were all already wet, it didn't really bother them. It was too late to worry about something so trivial.

"No, we came here to save Claudia. Until we can make sure she's okay, we can't…" Julis fell silent, staggering as she tried and failed to lift herself to her feet.

"A-are you okay?" Kirin asked.

"Ah, yeah… I'm fine." Julis held up a hand to reassure her, holding the other one against the ground to prop herself up.

During the fight, she had used several large-scale abilities in quick succession, and her prana seemed to be almost completely depleted. It would have been wise to conserve it as much as possible, given that they still had the semifinal tomorrow, but their situation had been such that she hadn't really been given much of a choice.

All of a sudden, her mobile began to ring.

"—! Ayato?!" she cried.

Her companions leaned forward to catch the conversation. Julis opened the air-window as quickly as her fingers could move, Ayato's weary face appearing before her.

"Julis, are you guys all right?"

"Well, it looks like we pulled through. But forget about us for a minute. What's going on on your end? Where are you now? Is Claudia…?" The questions came pouring out of her one after another.

"*We're at the hospital,*" Ayato replied. *"Claudia's—"*

*

It was close to midnight when Claudia opened her eyes.

"Where…am I?" she asked, her eyelids opening slowly.

"Not heaven, I'm afraid," Ayato, who had been waiting by her side the whole time, teased.

A smile rose to Claudia's lips as she tilted her neck toward him. "I know that much. With everything I've done, I'm destined for hell, not heaven."

"I guess you *must* be okay, if you can say things like that." Ayato breathed a sigh of relief. "We're in a special care unit in the hospital. There was a doctor here, just a short while ago, a healer…"

"…Ah, no wonder my chest feels better."

For Ayato, it had been his first time watching a healer at work. He couldn't help but be impressed by how effective the treatment had been. Still, given how much of the doctor's prana the process had consumed, he could understand why such techniques were only employed in the most serious of situations.

That was why, despite the fact that he himself had suffered considerable injuries of his own, he had received conventional medical treatment. That said, Director Jan Korbel had seen to everything himself, so he should probably be grateful, he mused.

"The healers here truly are excellent... Hatefully so." She spoke softly, but Ayato couldn't fail to catch her words.

"Can you tell me what's going on, Claudia?" he asked, his expression grave.

Claudia looked away, lowering her eyes. The room descended into a long, drawn-out silence.

Ayato decided to give her time, and as he had expected, she eventually relented: "What do you want to know?" she asked softly.

"Everything," Ayato replied without hesitation.

"...I see." She sighed in defeat, sitting up. "Very well. I can't say that you don't deserve an explanation. But you must have already realized it? That dying today, there, that was my one true wish." Claudia's voice rang with disappointment.

Her tone was enough to tell him beyond all doubt that she wasn't joking.

As she had guessed, Ayato had indeed realized it, somewhere deep inside. He hadn't wanted to believe it, hadn't wanted her to confirm his worst suspicions. Hearing it come from her own lips, he couldn't hide his shock.

"...Why on earth would you wish for something like that?" He had to force the words out.

Claudia gave him a dejected laugh. "I don't think you would understand. No, not just you. I don't think anyone on this planet, anyone but me, would be able to understand," she whispered, letting her eyes drift shut. "I was still a child when I received the Pan-Dora. Living through those nightmares every night, life seemed to lose all meaning and value... No matter how much you fight it, everyone dies one day. No matter how happy a life you might live, in the end, it doesn't add up to anything. There's no changing that. I came to realize—not through words or logic, but with my body—that it isn't how you live that's most important. It's how you die."

Ayato wanted to disagree with her, but he forced himself to remain silent.

At the very least, only someone who had experienced the nightmares caused by the Pan-Dora could hope to understand the meaning that lay behind her words.

"And then, one night, I met you, Ayato… The Pan-Dora introduced us, in my dreams."

"Me?"

Laetitia, it seemed, had been spot-on.

Claudia opened her eyes, her expression a mixture of sadness and embarrassment. "My hero, leaping into danger to protect me, fighting to save my life… But in the dream, I still ended up dying." Her moist eyes were staring into his own. "I'd been waiting for you, ever since I had that dream. Yearning for you… I suppose I fell in love with you…"

"Claudia…" Ayato was at a loss as to how to respond.

So instead, he urged her to continue. "It was today? That's what you saw?"

"Yes. In the middle of all that rain, in Seidoukan's harbor block, I took that blade for you, and I died in your arms… And the dream ended. I knew then what my wish was, the one dream that I wanted to come true, the vision that I wanted to make reality."

"…"

Ayato listened on in silence.

"I've died more than a thousand times since then, but never in a better way than that. No. The more I died, the more certain I became. I already knew the truth." Claudia paused there, letting out a self-deprecating laugh. "The Pan-Dora was behind everything."

"Huh…?"

"Do you remember what I told you, that it has the worst personality? Showing me such a vivid, ideal death…and making me fall in love with you… It's enjoyed itself, toying with my life."

"That's…" Ayato was at a loss for words.

"Do you want me to give you an example? I've been killed by so many people in my dreams, over and over again. People close to me, at that. There's been my mother and father, of course, Laetitia and Julis, Miss Sasamiya and Miss Toudou, even Eishirou Yabuki... But, Ayato, I've never been killed by you, not once. Doesn't that strike you as odd?"

"But if you knew what it was doing, then why...?"

"Hee-hee. Isn't it obvious?" Claudia asked with a soft laugh. "Even if you can look at it all logically, love isn't something that you can just make yourself stop feeling," she said with a smile, tears welling in her eyes. "My wish was to turn that dream into reality—that was all. I put everything I had into it. That's why I came to Seidoukan, why I became student council president, why I had you transferred here on a special scholarship, why I entered the Gryps, why I fanned the flames at Galaxy until they decided to send someone to kill me, everything... It was all to make that vision come true."

"...But it didn't," Ayato said, taking something wrapped in a handkerchief from his pocket.

It was the silver charm that Laetitia had entrusted him with and that he had in turn given to Claudia—split in two.

"According to Director Korbel, if it had been even a centimeter or so deeper, you might not have pulled through. This charm might have saved your life."

"That's... That's the kind of miracle you might expect in a cheap drama." Claudia laughed, before catching her breath. "To tell you the truth... I had a bad feeling about it, when you gave it to me. It didn't happen, in my dream."

So that was it, Ayato thought. *That's why she made that face.*

"...That's everything. Now, Ayato. Feel free to take me to task. I'm ready for it."

"Why would I do that?"

"Because... You know... Because I, thanks to no more than a foolish, selfish dream, used you, deceived you, and everyone else as well. I deserve to be punished." There was a slight tremble to her voice.

"..."

Ayato stood up in silence, walked over to the window, and pulled back the curtain.

The rain, it seemed, had come to an end, and the moon had come out to illuminate the city.

"Well... There *is* a part of me that can't help but feel upset. I mean, no matter how dear a wish it was for you, *I* wanted you to live," he said, staring up at the moon. "And it wasn't just me. I'm sure the others all felt the same way. Especially Julis. I can already imagine just how red with anger she'll be."

"...Yes."

At this, Ayato glanced over his shoulder, fixing her in his gaze. "But before that, there's something I want to ask you."

"There is?"

"Yes. What do you want to do after this, Claudia?"

"Huh? A-after this?" she repeated, glancing around nervously.

The question, it seemed, had taken her completely by surprise.

Ayato, having never seen her act that way before, found himself smiling in amusement. "That's right. Fortunately—although it feels strange to say this—we managed to completely shatter your dream this time."

"...You're relentless, aren't you?"

"Well, I'm angry, aren't I? But let's put that aside for the moment. I want you to tell me what you want to do now—your hopes, your wishes, that kind of thing."

"I don't know what to say... Why are you asking me that?" Claudia was unable to hide her confusion.

"Because I want to know more about you, of course, so that you don't ever do something like this again."

Claudia looked back at him blankly. "Are you saying...that you forgive me, Ayato?" she murmured in disbelief.

"No, not yet. I still want to get a few things off my chest first. But that's a separate matter. Before we get to that, I want to discuss with you what we're going to do from here on out."

"From here on out...?" she repeated, as if in a daze.

And then, she smiled, a smile so sad that she looked as if she might break down into tears at any moment. "I don't... How can I possibly have any idea…? I mean, I've lived my whole life waiting for today…! And now, now you're asking me about the future?"

"Then let's start thinking about it now," Ayato suggested.

"I-it isn't that simple…"

"You don't need to come to a decision right away. Dreams and wishes are things that pop up in our normal, everyday lives. So long as you keep moving, they'll come to you. That's what I think, at least."

"So long as I keep moving…"

"Right, but if it's the same kind of wish as last time, I'll have to stop you," Ayato added, half joking, half serious.

Claudia burst into laughter, as if she couldn't hold herself back any more. "It looks like you can be selfish, too!"

"We're pretty similar, I suppose."

Claudia's shoulders continued to shake with laughter for a long moment, until finally she brushed the tears from her face and glanced up at him. "All right. In that case, I'll… I'll keep moving," she said, suddenly reinvigorated.

With that, Ayato felt as if he could finally start putting the day's events behind him.

"…Thank you, Claudia," he said, taking her hand.

"Why are you thanking me?" she said with a soft laugh. "It's almost as if we've swapped places…" But she trailed off there, her body turning stiff.

"…Claudia?"

Her gaze was resting on her hand, placed within his own.

"N-no, I mean, it's nothing…!" Flustered, she pulled her hand away, spun around in her hospital bed—and fell crashing onto the floor.

"Ah… S-sorry." Though taken by surprise at her response, Ayato tried to apologize. They had been no more intimate than they usually were.

And yet, Claudia, having turned red all the way to her ears, glanced up at him bashfully.

Ayato had never seen this side of her before. Before he knew it, his heart was racing.

"U-um… Ayato?"

"Huh? Wh-what is it…?"

"Earlier, I think… I confessed my feelings to you, didn't I…?"

"Y-yeah…" He nodded.

"M-my thoughts were all over the place… T-try to put it out of your mind…"

"Huh?"

"I… I'd like to do it properly, next time… One day…," Claudia said, burying her face in her pillow.

"Ah… All right." Those were the only words that came to his lips.

"…"

"…"

They both descended into silence. After a while—Ayato didn't know how long—there came a knock at the door.

"Ayato, Claudia. Can we come in?" Julis said, her face projected on an air-window by the door.

Saya and Kirin were standing behind her.

Ayato turned to Claudia. "You'll have to explain everything to them now, too. And then, after that… Make sure you're ready for it, because we'll all give you a scolding together."

"Yes, I know. But still…" Claudia looked uneasy, but Ayato smiled back at her in reassurance.

"You'll be fine. They'll probably say the same kind of thing I did. In fact, I'm willing to bet on it," he responded.

Finally, Claudia nodded. She seemed to be wearing her usual smile—but no, there was something slightly different about it. "All right," she answered.

*

"Phew…" Claudia, finally left to herself in the moonlit hospital room, let out a deep sigh.

In the end, Julis and the others had given her a sound telling-off for upward of an hour.

Saya, in her usual simple and cool fashion; Kirin tenderly—and to

Claudia's surprise, with tears in her eyes. They took her to task for her selfishness and betrayal, but they were also relieved and overjoyed that she had survived. Even Julis, whose fury at hearing the truth had blazed like a wildfire, couldn't keep a tinge of sympathy from coming through in her voice.

"...I don't think I've ever been so thoroughly scolded before," Claudia said to herself.

Even so, she was grateful to them. They had all accepted what she had said, accepted *her.*

"What should I do from here...?" she murmured, echoing what Ayato had said a short while earlier.

The future stretching out in front of her was a terrifyingly blank swath of canvas.

How ironic, she thought, *for someone with the power of precognition.*

"Well, at any rate, I'll have to set things straight on that front first," Claudia murmured, pulling out her mobile from beside her pillow.

How many years had it been since she had called her by her own volition?

After a short moment, the face of her mother—Isabella—appeared in an air-window.

"To think that I would receive a phone call from you. I suppose miracles do happen," her mother said with her usual perfect smile and gentle voice. *"I'll hear you out."*

"First, I would like to thank you."

"*...For what?*" Isabella tilted her head to one side.

"I think that I've been able to grow a little, thanks to today."

Her mother, perhaps believing that she was being sarcastic, narrowed her eyes. "*...You might have pulled through this time, but there won't be any second chances.*"

"Yes, I understand that. Which is why...I surrender."

"*...Surrender?*" she repeated suspiciously.

"This isn't a trap, and I'm not trying to trick you. I'm saying that I admit that I've lost."

"You can't possibly be saying that you're valuing your life now, after it's come to this?"

"That's exactly it... I do value my life. I'm just as surprised as you are."

"..."

Claudia could feel the intensity of her mother's gaze through the air-window as she tried to sound her out.

There was little wonder for her to act that way. It was only natural for her to be suspicious, given that the person she was dealing with, usually so obstinate, had raised the white flag so suddenly. Especially so, given that that person had practically already won from a tactical standpoint, albeit not a strategic one.

"Even if I did believe you, do you really think that Galaxy will agree to lay down their arms? It won't end here, not now that it's come to this. You're the one who created this situation, after all."

"Yes, I understand that, too. Our negotiations can start now," Claudia said, turning back to her mobile.

"The time for negotiations has long since passed...," Isabella began, before falling silent.

"I've just sent you some data. Please, take a look."

"This..." Isabella's eyes opened wide in astonishment.

"Did you think that the knowledge I gleaned from the cost demanded by the Pan-Dora related only to the Varda-Vaos? What I've sent you is confidential, of course, information relating to Queenvale and Le Wolfe. Please, think of it as a present."

"...A present?" Isabella's eyes glowed. She was clearly already running through how the information might be used.

That was just to be expected. A top executive at an integrated enterprise foundation wouldn't turn a blind eye to something that might strengthen their organization's ability to turn a profit.

"From now on, I'll provide all information like this to Galaxy. What do you think? Is that a good enough position to consider opening negotiations?"

"...Very well," Isabella said after pondering it for a long moment. *"I'll look into this. Until then, you won't need to worry about your safety."*

"Thank you. And, Mother...?"

"*...Yes?*"

"I know this is sudden, but do you mind if I ask why you joined Galaxy?"

Given that her father, Nicholas, belonged to the Enfield family, which had been heavily involved in the Reconstruction in Europe after the Invertia, it made sense that he would work for the foundation. Her mother, however, was the kind of person one could find in any large city and had no obvious connection to the group.

"*Why do you want to know?*" Isabella seemed to be taken aback by her daughter's sudden question.

"I just thought it might be interesting, if I was to join Galaxy one day...and take your place," Claudia said with a grin.

It was just an idle fancy. Being a Genestella, it would be all but impossible for her to rise to the same executive rank as her mother, and she wouldn't consider for a second, not even as a joke, being subject to any sort of mental adjustment program.

However, putting all that aside, it would be interesting, she thought, if that option was available to her.

"*Hee-hee, hee-hee-hee-hee! How delightful! But what on earth has come over you, Claudia?*" Isabella said, laughing and breaking out into a naturally happy smile, the likes of which Claudia couldn't remember ever having seen before. "*Very well. If one day you and I can stand shoulder to shoulder...I'll tell you,*" she finished, and with that, the air-window turned black.

After a short moment, Claudia collapsed onto the bed, beaming up at the ceiling. "I see. So she thinks that there *is* a possibility...," she murmured, before letting her eyes drift shut in contentment.

The feeling that had taken hold of her wasn't unpleasant.

"...Ah, yes," she murmured, opening her eyes. There was someone else she had to thank, and complain to, she remembered, reaching again for her mobile.

"Hello, Laetitia. I don't suppose I could have a moment of your time?"

EPILOGUE

Eishirou was sitting idly in the treetops, staring up at the moon, high in the now-clear sky.

How much time had he been idling away like this? he wondered, before letting out a deep, tired sigh. "Ahhh, now I've gone and done it..."

He had gone too far this time.

He didn't regret what he had done, but only a fool wouldn't be able to see the coming reckoning. After all, he had practically stabbed his father in the back.

Well, strictly speaking, he had stabbed him on the sly, but there was no way that he wouldn't have been noticed.

"Maybe I should just leave it all behind..."

But if he did that, he would have to leave the academy, too, and that was something he would definitely end up regretting.

No matter how far he searched, he doubted he would find another city as crazy as this one, and it was impossible to grow tired of watching all the things that Ayato, Julis, and Claudia got themselves into... Not to mention the club president.

"But what can I do now?"

Eishirou, who normally tried to live his life as leisurely as possible, found himself racking his brains, searching for an answer—when his mobile began to ring.

"Ugh..." The sound leaked out of him as soon as he saw the number, but he couldn't afford to let it keep ringing.

He opened an air-window, Bujinsai's taciturn face appearing before him.

"Hey there, Pops. I was really sorry to hear that the mission didn't work out."

Even Eishirou was impressed at just how casually he was able to talk, given the situation.

"Be quiet. Do you know just how much damage you've done to us, to our name?" Judging by his tone, his father was clearly in a foul mood, but there was no sign of his thorough beating at Ayato's hands.

"What's all this? I don't have a clue what you're going on about...," Eishirou responded, playing dumb.

"Where do you want me to start...? What's most galling is that you gave Eika's location to that kid from Jie Long."

It looked like his father knew everything.

Eishirou had indeed forwarded Alema everything he had about the Yabuki's positions, including the whereabouts of Eika and the other healers.

"It's one thing to defy me, but to rat out your sister like that... My disgust for you goes beyond words."

"But they weren't injured too badly, were they?"

Alema had already been seriously wounded herself. No matter how weak the clan's healers might be when it came to fighting for themselves, the worst that Alema could have done to them would have been to knock them out cold in a surprise attack.

"Nonetheless, it's unforgivable. According to the clan's rules, I ought to go over there and sever that head of yours right now...," he said, making a sour face. *"But unfortunately, our employers seem to be quite happy with you."*

"Huh...?"

His father's words came out of the blue.

"Galaxy? With me?"

"So we can't touch you. But don't you ever think about coming home again."

He had no desire to do so in the first place, so that wouldn't be a problem.

"All right. I'll engrave that on my heart."

"...*Hmph!*" Bujinsai continued to glare back at him, until, finally, the air-window snapped shut.

Eishirou sat there in baffled silence. Galaxy's satisfaction with him was incomprehensible.

Instead of punishing a pawn that had turned against its masters, they had instead saved his skin.

He remained that way for a long while, pondering why they might have done that for him, but no matter how he tried to approach the problem, he couldn't hit on even one logical answer.

There was only one possibility, but it didn't make any sense.

"Nah, that can't be right..."

No matter how much she might have been concerned for her daughter's safety, one of Galaxy's highest executives wouldn't go that far. It went against everything the position called for.

"...Oh well. I guess I'd better head back," he muttered, casting the thought out of his mind as he leaped down from the treetops.

*

"...Yes, yes, that goes without saying! You should do your best, too, and be sure to make it to the final!" a voice echoed from just outside the room.

Before long, Laetitia opened the door fully, striding back into the office with a strangely satisfied expression.

She was even humming to herself.

"You look pleased, Laetitia. Good news?" Ernest asked.

Taken by surprise, Laetitia, her face turning as red as a fully ripe apple, shook her head from side to side. "I-it's nothing! R-really!"

"...I see. Well, in any event, this furor surrounding Miss Enfield seems to have resolved itself. Sinodomius has confirmed that the Nights have left the city." Ernest watched her with a faint smile, putting his hands together and crossing his fingers.

"O-oh, really? That's good to hear."

"I take it that her injuries aren't too serious, then?"

"She was seen to by a healer, so there's no need to worry about that… Ah!"

Ernest tried to suppress his mirth at having so easily coaxed the information out of her. "There's no need to hide the fact that you've been in contact with her. You didn't say anything that you shouldn't have, I assume?"

Laetitia wasn't that foolish. She understood that regular communications could be listened in on by Sinodomius, and she wouldn't have said anything that could be used against her.

"O-of course not…," she mumbled, the words so muffled as to be almost incomprehensible.

She looked, more than anything else, embarrassed.

"Ah, and tomorrow's match—well, today's, I guess. Anyway, it seems that we've already won our semifinals bout by default."

"Oh… I see."

"There was no helping it, given the situation. The Executive Committee must have taken it as a last resort… Fortunately for us, we'll now be able to enter the final in perfect condition. I do wonder about our opponents, though…"

"…"

Laetitia absorbed his words in silence, her expression grave.

They might have overcome this incident, but Team Enfield's next opponents were incredibly powerful.

"There's every possibility that it will be Team Yellow Dragon that we face in the final. That *is* what the odds would suggest."

Jie Long's Team Yellow Dragon was practically the complete antithesis of Ernest and Laetitia's Team Lancelot. It might be an incredibly powerful assortment of fighters, centered around Xiaohui Wu, the famous Hagun Seikun, but the way Ernest saw them, they were completely devoid of charm. He just couldn't see anything interesting about a single one of them.

"As for me, I would prefer that Team Enfield make it through."

"Of course they will!" Laetitia answered confidently. "They'll make it! I'm sure of it!"

"Laetitia..." Though somewhat surprised by her assurance, Ernest nodded back at her. "Yes, you're right. I'll be looking forward to it."

At any rate, they would know for sure by this time tomorrow.

Ernest tightened his linked fingers, as if to smolder the flames burning deep inside him.

*

"Yes, well done. It's turned out wonderfully, Alema," Xinglou said cheerfully, her small legs shaking giddily from atop her oversized chair. "Thanks to you, tomorrow's match should be very fun indeed."

They were in Xinglou's audience chamber at Jie Long Seventh Institute.

"...I'M NOT VERY PROUD OF IT MYSELF, THOUGH." Alema, her body covered in bandages, let out a pitiful sigh.

She had achieved her goals, but Bujinsai had soundly defeated her. And what was more, he had left her in her present state.

"Now, now, don't take it to heart. I did tell you that his Void Tide techniques would be a hassle, didn't I? Even among my disciples, probably only Xiaohui and Fuyuka would be able to do anything about them."

"IS IT OKAY TO CALL FUYUKA YOUR DISCIPLE? SHE'S ONLY A GUEST HERE."

"She thinks of herself that way, so I don't mind," Xinglou said with a dry laugh.

Alema stared at Xinglou in astonishment, before suddenly remembering something that Bujinsai had said to her.

"RIGHT, I HEARD SOMETHING EARLIER."

"Oh?"

"Is it true that you're not even half as strong as you used to be?"

At this, Xinglou broke into a broad grin. "Oh, did the Yabuki head say that?"

"I don't know if I really believe him, though."

Of course, it would all be so much more interesting if it was true.

Still, despite having seen for herself only a fragment of Xinglou's true strength, she couldn't quite bring herself to fully believe him.

"Let's see, he's half correct, I suppose."

"Half?"

"In my current body, I'm probably only thirty or forty percent of what I was during my prime, at least as far as martial arts are concerned. However, my abilities and techniques are a different matter. I'm overflowing with mana now, and my power and accuracy go beyond anything I've ever had before."

"...I see."

Though finally able to believe it, Alema found herself reminded of just how powerful the young girl sitting before her really was.

The two had sparred together countless times, but Alema hadn't seen her use those techniques even once.

"Ah, it's getting my blood pumping just thinking about it...!"

"Oh-ho, you never change." Xinglou nodded in satisfaction before clapping her hands together. "Yes, that's it. Shall I show you something as a reward for your good work?"

"Oh, like what?"

"A little plan I'm working on for the Lindvolus. If things work out, maybe I'll let you in on it." Xinglou beckoned for her to come closer. "You see..."

"Heh-heh..." As she heard her out, Alema broke into an uncontrollable grin. "Awesome! That sounds amazing!"

"Doesn't it just? I've already selected several people for it. Well, they won't do anything until the new year."

"Ha-ha! I can't wait!" Alema clenched her hands together.

“Ah, but I should warn you. Don’t let Hufeng know. If he was to find out, he’d stop at nothing to bring it to an end.”

“GOT IT!”

At that moment—

“Master, there’s something I want to discuss… Oh. Has something happened?” Hufeng, having entered the room unannounced, glanced back and forth between the two in confusion.

“No, nothing to worry about,” Xinglou answered. “So… What is it?”

At this, Hufeng put his right fist in his left palm in a gesture of obeisance.

“I would like your permission to use that Orga Lux in tomorrow’s semifinal!”

AFTERWORD

Hello again, Yuu Miyazaki here.

I've got so much to announce this time that I ended up writing four whole pages for this afterword, so I'd like to apologize in advance for going on and on.

All right. Let's start with what happened in this volume. This will contain minor spoilers, so those of you who haven't finished reading should look away now!

I'm so happy to have finally been able to give you a story centered around Claudia. The tone of this volume is somewhat darker than the previous ones, as is Claudia's characterization, and her story is somewhat different than those of the other heroines. Still, it's one that I've been wanting to write ever since I first introduced her, and it's a great joy to have finally been able to do so.

On the other hand, given that so many of my readers have told me just how much they love her as a character, I must admit that I felt a little uneasy putting it all to paper. I hope that you can all continue to be just as fond of her as you have been up till now.

While this volume focuses on Claudia, there are several other important plot threads and themes, such as the relationships between the IEFs and students, between parents and children, and between individuals and the schools' intelligence networks. These scenes were particularly fun to write.

In the next volume, number ten, we'll finally make it to the climax of the Gryps.

Expect it to be fully loaded with all kinds of battles!

Once again, okiura's cover art is a masterpiece! Julis and Sylvia, Saya and Miluše, and now Claudia and Laetitia! Two beautiful blondes! And the illustration of Ayato and Eishirou is also fantastic! I could feel myself getting giddy the first time I saw it! Not only does okiura draw the girls so adorably, he makes the boys look so cool as well!

The third volume of Ningen's manga adaptation of *The Asterisk War* serialized in *Monthly Comic Alive* should be hitting shelves around the same time as this book. The manga adaptation has already passed the end of the first volume of the original and is moving briskly into the second. Ningen's depiction of Kirin is so lovely! Please take a look at it!

On top of that, the second volume of Akane Shou's manga adaptation of *The Asterisk War: The Wings of Queenvale* in *Bessatsu Shōnen* magazine will be available soon, too! Chloe is on the cover! And her other team members are all there, too! Several characters from the original pop-up, as well, so please take a look at that one as well!

Now, for some extra news that I'm especially proud to announce.

Anime!

That's right, the anime adaptation of the *The Asterisk War* will start airing on October 3! This volume should hit shelves around September 25, so only around a week after that. I can't wait to watch it! I've attended meetings to discuss the script and spoken to so many people about it. I'm really impressed by just how many people are involved in putting something like this together. I've picked up so many business cards! It really is wonderful, so please be sure to watch it!

Game!

Yes, a video game, tentatively title *The Asterisk War: Phoenix Festa*, has been announced! I've watched Ms. Kakuma, who voices Julis, play a bit of it, and I've even been able to have a go myself! When I first heard about the project, I was so stunned to hear that it would be an action game. There should be more information coming out soon, so stay tuned!

Merchandise!

Coinciding with the anime, there should be all kinds of merchandise coming out as well! It'd make me so happy if you could take a look at them!

Last but not least, I'd like to thank everyone who did so much to help me again this time around.

Once again, I'd like to thank my editor, Mr. I, for continuing to put up with me. And of course, to Mr. S and Mr. O, and everyone else in the editorial department, everyone involved with the anime and the game, and, of course, to my readers for your fantastic support. Thank you all so much.

I hope to see you all again next time!

Yuu Miyazaki
August 2015

SEIDOUKAN ACADEMY

SILAS NORMAN

A former companion of Lester's. Attacked Ayato with Allekant's backing but was defeated.

ALLEKANT ACADÉMIE

SHUUMA SAKON

Student council president of Allekant Académie.

ERNESTA KÜHNE

Creator of Ardy and Rimcy.

CAMILLA PARETO

Ernesta's research partner.

ARDY (AR-D)—"ABSOLUTE REFUSAL" DEFENDED MODEL

Autonomous puppet. Fought alongside Rimcy during the Phoenix.

RIMCY (RM-C)—"RUINOUS MIGHT" CANNON MODEL

Autonomous puppet. Fought alongside Ardy during the Phoenix.

HILDA JANE ROWLANDS

One of the greatest geniuses in Allekant's history. Also known as the Great Scholar, Magnum Opus.

NARCISSE PERROY

Vice president of the Ferrovius faction. Architect of the Gran Colosseo.

LE WOLFE BLACK INSTITUTE

DIRK EBERWEIN

Student council president of Le Wolfe Black Institute.

KORONA KASHIMARU

Secretary to Le Wolfe's student council president.

ORPHELIA LANDLUFEN

Two-time champion of the Lindvolus and the most powerful Strega in Asterisk.

IRENE URZAIZ

Priscilla's elder sister. Under Dirk's control. Alias the Vampire Princess, Lamilexia.

PRISCILLA URZAIZ

Irene's younger sister. A regenerative.

WERNHER

A member of Grimalkin's Gold Eyes. Kidnapped Flora.

MORITZ

Appeared in the Phoenix, where he was miserably defeated by Ardy.

GERD

Moritz's tag partner. Defeated by Rimcy.

JIE LONG SEVENTH INSTITUTE

XINGLOU FAN

Jie Long's top-ranked fighter and student council president. Alias Immanent Heaven, Ban'yuu Tenra.

XIAOHUI WU

Jie Long's second-ranked fighter and Xinglou Fan's top disciple.

CECILY WONG

Hufeng Zhao's former tag partner, with whom she became a runner-up at the Phoenix.

HUFENG ZHAO

An exceptional martial artist often entrusted with secretarial tasks by Xinglou Fan, who always gives him something to worry about.

SHENYUN LI & SHENHUA LI

Twin brother and sister. Defeated by Ayato and Julis during the Phoenix.

SONG & LUO

Fought against Ayato and Julis in the fifth round of the Phoenix.

SAINT GALLARDWORTH ACADEMY

ERNEST FAIRCLOUGH

Gallardworth's top-ranked fighter and student council president.

LAETITIA BLANCHARD

Gallardworth's second-ranked fighter and student council vice president.

PERCIVAL GARDNER

Gallardworth's fifth-ranked fighter and student council secretary.

ELLIOT FORSTER

Fought with Doroteo during the Phoenix, with whom he advanced to the semifinals.

DOROTEO LEMUS

Together with Elliot, defeated by Ayato and Julis during the semifinals of the Phoenix.

QUEENVALE ACADEMY FOR YOUNG LADIES

SYLVIA LYYNEHEYM

Queenvale's top-ranked fighter, student council president, and popular idol.

MILUŠE

Rusalka's leader. Vocalist and lead guitarist.

PÄIVI

Rusalka's drummer.

MONICA

Rusalka's bassist.

TUULIA

Rusalka's rhythm guitarist.

MAHULENA

Rusalka's keyboardist.

YUZUHI RENJOUJI

Studies the Amagiri Shinmei Style Archery Techniques. Acquainted with Ayato.

VIOLET WEINBERG

Alias the Witch of Demolition, Overliezel.

OTHERS

HARUKA AMAGIRI

Ayato's elder sister. Her whereabouts had been unaccounted for, but she was discovered in a deep sleep.

HELGA LINDWALL

Head of Stjarnagarm.

MADIATH MESA

Chairman of the Festa Executive Committee.

DANILO BERTONI

Former Chairman of the Festa Executive Committee. Died several years ago.

URSULA SVEND

Sylvia's teacher. Her body has been taken over by Varda.

JAN KORBEL

Director of the hospital treating Haruka.

GUSTAVE MALRAUX

One of seventy-seven individuals involved in the Jade Twilight Incident, an act of terrorism.

MICO YANASE

Announcer at the Phoenix.

PHAM THI TRAM

Commentator at the Phoenix.

FLORA KLEMM

A young girl from the orphanage Julis is supporting.

SISTER THERESE

The representative from the orphanage Julis is supporting.

JOLBERT

Julis's elder brother and the king of Lieseltania.

MARIA

Queen of Lieseltania.

SOUICHI SASAMIYA

Saya's father. Lost most of his body in an accident and appears as a hologram.

KAYA SASAMIYA

Saya's mother.

NICHOLAS ENFIELD

Claudia's father.

KOUICHIROU TOUDOU

Kirin's uncle. Planned to use her to boost his career at his integrated enterprise foundation, but failed.

RIKKA: THE ACADEMY CITY ON THE WATER

QUEENVALE ACADEMY FOR YOUNG LADIES

Their school crest is the Idol, a nameless goddess of hope. The culture here is bright and showy, and in addition to fighting ability, another criterion for admission is good looks. It is the smallest of the six schools.

COMMERCIAL AREA

MAIN STAGE

CENTRAL DISTRICT

ADMINISTRATIVE AREA

LE WOLFE BLACK INSTITUTE

Their school crest of Crossed Swords signifies military might. They have a tremendously belligerent school culture that actually encourages their students to duel. Owing to this, their relationship with Gallardworth is strained.

ITY TOWN "RIKKA"

SEIDOUKAN ACADEMY

Their school crest is the Red Lotus, the emblem of an indomitable spirit. The school culture values individuality, and rules are fairly relaxed. Traditionally, they have many Stregas and Dantes among the students.

SAINT GALLARDWORTH ACADEMY

Their school crest is the Ring of Light, symbolizing order. Their rigid culture values discipline and loyalty above all else, and in principle, even duels are forbidden. This puts them on poor terms with Le Wolfe.

An academic metropolis, floating atop the North Kanto Mass-Impact Crater Lake. Its overall shape is a regular hexagon, and from each vertex, a school campus protrudes like a bastion. A main avenue runs from each school straight to the center, giving rise to the nickname Asterisk.

This city is the site of the world's largest fighting event, the Festa, and is a major tourist destination.

Although Asterisk is technically a part of Japan, it is governed directly by multiple integrated enterprise foundations and has complete extraterritoriality.

OUTER RESIDENTIAL DISTRICT

JIE LONG SEVENTH INSTITUTE

Their school crest is the Yellow Dragon, the mightiest of the four gods, signifying sovereignty. Bureaucracy clashes with a laissez-faire attitude, making the school culture rather chaotic. The largest of the six schools, they incorporate a Far Eastern atmosphere into almost everything.

ALLEKANT ACADÉMIE

Their school crest is the Dark Owl, a symbol of wisdom and the messenger of Minerva. Their guiding principle is absolute meritocracy, and students are divided into research and practical classes. They are unparalleled in meteoric engineering technology.

THE WORLD OF *THE ASTERISK WAR* GLOSSARY

THE INVERTIA

A mysterious disaster that befell Earth in the twentieth century. Meteors fell all over the world for three days and three nights, destroying many cities. As a result, the strength of existing nations declined considerably, and a new form of economic power known as "integrated enterprise foundations" took their place.

A previously unknown element called *mana* was extracted from the meteorites, leading to advances in scientific technology as well as a new type of human with extraordinary powers, called Genestella.

The Invertia was undetected by all the observatories in the world, and the destruction it caused was actually much less than ordinary meteors, so the pervading theory is that it did not consist of normal meteors.

INTEGRATED ENTERPRISE FOUNDATION

A new type of economic entity formed by corporations that merged to overcome the choatic economic situation following the Invertia. Their power far surpasses that of the diminished nations.

There used to be eight IEFs, but there are currently six: Galaxy, EP (Elliott-Pound), Jie Long, Solnage, Frauenlob, and W&W (Warren & Warren). They vie for advantage over one another and effectively control the world. Each one sponsors an academy in Asterisk.

THE FESTA

A fighting tournament where students compete, held in Asterisk, and operated by the IEFs. Each cycle, or "season," consists of three events: the tag match (Phoenix) in the summer of the first year, the team battle (Gryps) in the fall of the second year, and the individual match (Lindvolus) in the winter of the third year. Victory is achieved by destroying the opponent's school crest, and the rules are set forth in the Stella Carta. As the event is held for entertainment, acts of deliberate cruelty and attacks intended to cause death or injury can be penalized.

The event is the most popular one in the world, with matches broadcast internationally. The IEFs prioritize economic success and growth above all else, so the direction of the Festa has always been driven by the majority demand of consumers. (This is why the fighters are students—viewers want to see beautiful boys and girls fight one another.) Some speak out against the Festa on ethical grounds, but under the rule of the IEFs, those voices have fallen from justified dissent to unpopular opinion.

The cultures of the different schools veer to extremes, which is also by design, for the sake of the Festa.

THE STELLA CARTA

Rules that apply strictly to all the students of Asterisk. Those who violate these rules are harshly penalized, sometimes by expulsion. If a school is found to have been involved, the administration can also be subject to penalty. The Stella Carta has been amended several times in the past. The most important items are as follows:

- Combat between students of Asterisk is permitted only insofar as the intent is to destroy the other's school crest.
- Each student of Asterisk shall be eligible to participate in the Festa between the ages of 13 and 22, a period spanning ten years.
- Each student of Asterisk shall participate in the Festa no more than three times.

MANA

A previously unknown element that was brought to Earth by the Invertia. By now, it can be found all over the world. It responds to the will of living beings who meet certain criteria, incorporating surrounding elements to form objects and create phenomena.

GENESTELLA

A new type of human being, born after regular human children were exposed to mana. With an aura known as *prana*, they possess physical abilities far beyond those of ordinary humans. Genestella who can tap into mana without special equipment are called Stregas (female) and Dantes (male).

Discrimination against Genestella is a pervasive social problem, and many students come to Asterisk to escape this. (The negative bias against Genestella is one reason why opposition to the Festa is in the minority.)

PRANA

A kind of aura unique to Genestella. Stregas and Dantes deplete prana as they use their powers. They lose consciousness if they run out of prana, but it can simply be replenished with time. The manipulation of prana is a basic skill among Genestella, and by focusing it, they can increase offensive or defensive strength. This is especially effective for defense, which explains why serious injuries among Asterisk students are rare despite the common use of weapons.

METEORIC ENGINEERING

A field of science that studies mana and the meteorites from the Invertia. Many mysteries remain pertaining to mana, but experimentation on manadite has advanced significantly. Fueled by the abundance of rare metals found in the meteorites, manadite research has yielded a large variety of practical applications.

MANADITE

A special ore made of crystallized mana. If stress is applied, it can store or retain specific elemental patterns. Before the Invertia, it did not exist on Earth, and it must be extracted from meteorites. Manadite is used in Lux activators, as well as manufactured products developed through meteoric engineering.

LUX

A type of weapon with a manadite core. Records of elemental patterns are stored in pieces of manadite and re-created using activators. By gathering mana from the surroundings, they can create blades or projectiles of light. Mana also acts as the energy source for Lux weapons.

URM-MANADITE

A name for exceptionally pure manadite, much rarer than ordinary manadite. Luxes using urm-manadite are known as Orga Luxes. Urm-manadite crystals come in myriad colors and shapes, and no two are the same. They are said to have minds of their own.

ORGA LUX

A weapon using urm-manadite as its core. Many of them have special powers, but using them takes a toll—a certain "cost." The weapons themselves have something akin to a sentient will, and unsuitable users cannot even touch the weapon. Suitability is measured by means of a compatibility rating.

Most Orga Luxes are owned by the IEFs and are entrusted to the schools of Asterisk for the purpose of lending them to students with high compatibility ratings.

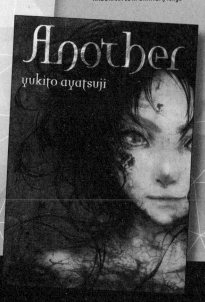

PREPARE TO ACCELERATE
WITH AN ACTION-PACKED CYBER-THRILLER FROM
THE BESTSELLING AUTHOR OF SWORD ART ONLINE!
ACCEL WORLD, VOL. 1–11
LIGHT NOVEL SERIES
REKI KAWAHARA
ILLUSTRATION BY HIMA
ACCEL WORLD
01 KUROYUKIHIME'S RETURN
THE RED STORM PRINCESS
ACCEL WORLD, VOL. 1–7
MANGA SERIES
ACCEL WORLD
Art: Hiroyuki Aigamo
Original Story: Reki Kawahara
Character Design: HIMA

Death doesn't stop a video game-loving shut-in from going on adventures and fighting monsters!

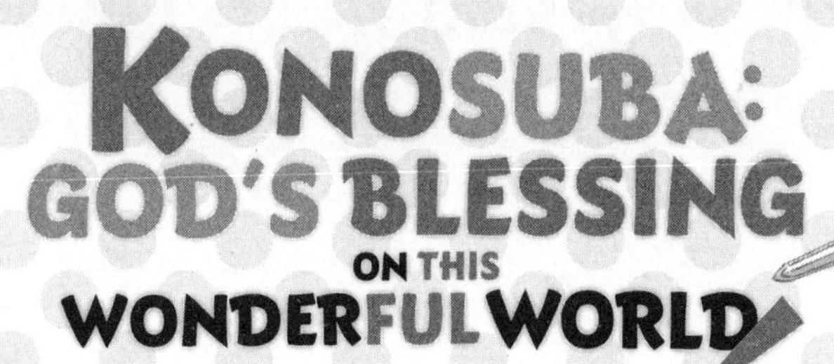

WATCH ON crunchyroll
www.crunchyroll.com/the-asterisk-war

Read the light novel that inspired the hit anime series!
Re:ZeRo
-Starting Life in Another World-
Also be sure to check out the manga series!
AVAILABLE NOW!
Yen Press
YEN ON
www.YenPress.com
Re:Zero Kara Hajimeru Isekai Seikatsu
© Tappei Nagatsuki, Daichi Matsuse / KADOKAWA CORPORATION
© Tappei Nagatsuki Illustration: Shinichirou Otsuka/ KADOKAWA CORPORATION